Kenice

Kenice Williams

Kenice Williams

Williams

Winter Tales from the Tree House

Magic Tree House® Books

#1: Dinosaurs Before Dark
#2: The Knight at Dawn
#3: Mummies in the Morning
#4: Pirates Past Noon
#5: Night of the Ninjas
#6: Afternoon on the Amazon
#7: Sunset of the Sabertooth
#8: Midnight on the Moon
#9: Dolphins at Daybreak
#10: Ghost Town at Sundown
#11: Lions at Lunchtime
#12: Polar Bears Past Bedtime
#13: Vacation Under the Volcano
#14: Day of the Dragon King
#15: Viking Ships at Sunrise
#16: Hour of the Olympics
#17: Tonight on the *Titanic*
#18: Buffalo Before Breakfast
#19: Tigers at Twilight
#20: Dingoes at Dinnertime
#21: Civil War on Sunday
#22: Revolutionary War on Wednesday
#23: Twister on Tuesday
#24: Earthquake in the Early Morning
#25: Stage Fright on a Summer Night
#26: Good Morning, Gorillas
#27: Thanksgiving on Thursday
#28: High Tide in Hawaii

Merlin Missions

#29: Christmas in Camelot
#30: Haunted Castle on Hallows Eve
#31: Summer of the Sea Serpent
#32: Winter of the Ice Wizard
#33: Carnival at Candlelight
#34: Season of the Sandstorms
#35: Night of the New Magicians
#36: Blizzard of the Blue Moon
#37: Dragon of the Red Dawn
#38: Monday with a Mad Genius
#39: Dark Day in the Deep Sea
#40: Eve of the Emperor Penguin
#41: Moonlight on the Magic Flute
#42: A Good Night for Ghosts
#43: Leprechaun in Late Winter
#44: A Ghost Tale for Christmas Time
#45: A Crazy Day with Cobras
#46: Dogs in the Dead of Night

Magic Tree House® Fact Trackers

Dinosaurs
Knights and Castles
Mummies and Pyramids
Pirates
Rain Forests
Space
Titanic
Twisters and Other Terrible Storms
Dolphins and Sharks
Ancient Greece and the Olympics
American Revolution
Sabertooths and the Ice Age
Pilgrims
Ancient Rome and Pompeii
Tsunamis and Other Natural Disasters
Polar Bears and the Arctic
Sea Monsters
Penguins and Antarctica
Leonardo da Vinci
Ghosts
Leprechauns and Irish Folklore
Rags and Riches: Kids in the Time of Charles Dickens
Snakes and Other Reptiles
NEW! Dog Heroes

More Magic Tree House®

Games and Puzzles from the Tree House

MAGIC TREE HOUSE®
MERLIN MISSIONS

Winter Tales from the Tree House

Includes **Winter of the Ice Wizard** and **Blizzard of the Blue Moon**

by Mary Pope Osborne
illustrated by Sal Murdocca

A STEPPING STONE BOOK™
Random House New York

For Sal Murdocca, Wizard of Wondrous Art
—from *Winter of the Ice Wizard*

To Elwood Smith, who long ago in New York City
inspired me to write for children
—from *Blizzard of the Blue Moon*

Grateful acknowledgment is made to Pantheon Books, a division of Random House, Inc., for permission to reprint an excerpt from "The Unicorn in Captivity" from *The Unicorn and Other Poems* by Anne Morrow Lindbergh, copyright © 1956 by Anne Morrow Lindbergh, renewed 1984 by Anne Morrow Lindbergh. Reprinted by permission of Pantheon Books, a division of Random House, Inc.

Visit us on the Web!
MagicTreeHouse.com
randomhouse.com/kids

Educators and librarians, for a variety of teaching tools, visit us at
randomhouse.com/teachers

Library of Congress Cataloging-in-Publication Data is available upon request.
ISBN: 978-0-375-97242-3 (trade)

Printed in the United States of America

10 9 8 7 6 5 4 3 2 1

Random House Children's Books supports the First Amendment and celebrates the right to read.

CONTENTS

Winter of the Ice Wizard

Dear Reader,

Winter of the Ice Wizard is the fourth "Merlin Mission" in the Magic Tree House series. In these books, Merlin the magician sends Jack and Annie on their tree house adventures to mythical lands.

In the first Merlin Mission, Christmas in Camelot, Jack and Annie journey to the Otherworld to find a magical cauldron that holds the Water of Memory and Imagination. Then in Haunted Castle on Hallows Eve, they rescue the stolen Diamond of Destiny with the help of their friend Teddy. In Summer of the Sea Serpent, Jack and Annie travel to an enchanted seacoast, where they find the hidden Sword of Light with Teddy and a seal girl named Kathleen.

Now, on the first day of winter, Jack and Annie are about to head out on another magical mission. They invite you to join them. But be sure to wear warm clothes and snow boots. You're going to a very cold land where very weird things happen. . . .

Mary Pope Osborne

The fetters shall break
And the wolf run free.
Secret things I know
And onward see.
—From *The Poetic Edda*

CHAPTER ONE

Winter Solstice

A cold wind rattled the windowpanes. But inside the house, it was warm and cozy. Jack and Annie were making Christmas cookies with their mom. Jack pressed a star-shaped cookie cutter into the dough.

"Hey, it's snowing outside," said Annie.

Jack looked out the window. Huge snowflakes were falling from the late-afternoon sky.

"You want to go out?" asked Annie.

"Not really. It'll be dark soon," said Jack.

"That's right," said their mom. "Today's the first day of winter. It's the shortest day of the year."

Jack's heart skipped a beat. "You mean it's the *winter solstice*?" he said.

"Yes," said their mom.

Annie gasped. "The winter solstice?" she said.

"Yes . . . ," their mom said, puzzled.

Jack and Annie looked at each other. Last summer, Merlin the magician had called for their help on the *summer* solstice. Maybe he would need them again today!

Jack put down the cookie cutter and wiped his hands on a towel. "Actually, Mom, it might be fun to play in the snow for just a few minutes," he said.

"Whatever you want," their mom said. "Just dress warmly. I'll finish up with the cookies and put them in the oven."

"Thanks!" said Jack. He and Annie raced to the closet and pulled on their boots. They threw on jackets, scarves, gloves, and caps.

"Be home before dark," their mom said.

"We will!" called Jack.

"Bye, Mom!" Annie shouted.

Jack and Annie slipped out of their house into the snowy cold. Their boots squeaked as they ran across their white yard and headed toward the Frog Creek woods.

At the edge of the woods, Jack stopped. He couldn't believe how beautiful the trees looked. White powder covered the branches of the hemlocks and pines.

"Look," said Annie. She pointed to two pairs of footprints that led out to the road and then back into the woods. "Somebody else has been here."

"It looks like they were walking out of the woods—but turned back," said Jack. "Let's hurry!" If the magic tree house *had* come back today, he didn't want anyone else finding it first!

Jack and Annie walked quickly through the woods, following the two sets of footprints.

"Stop!" said Annie. She pulled Jack behind a tree. "Over there!"

Through the falling snow, Jack saw two people in long, dark cloaks. They were hurrying toward a tall oak—and high in the oak was the magic tree house!

"Oh, no!" said Jack.

The tree house *was* back! And someone else had found it!

"Hey!" Jack yelled. "Stop!" The tree house had come for him and Annie—no one else!

Jack started running. Annie followed. Jack slipped and fell in the snow, but he scrambled up and kept going. By the time he and Annie got to the tree house, the two people had climbed up the rope ladder and disappeared inside.

"Come out!" Jack yelled.

"This is *our* tree house!" shouted Annie.

Two kids poked their heads out of the tree house window. They both looked like they were about thirteen years old. The boy had tousled red hair and freckles. The girl had sea-blue eyes and long, curly black hair. Their cheeks were rosy from the cold. They laughed when they saw Jack and Annie.

"Excellent!" said the boy. "We came to find you, but you have found us instead."

"Teddy!" cried Annie. "Kathleen! Hi!"

Teddy was the young sorcerer who worked with Morgan in her library in Camelot. Kathleen was the enchanted selkie girl who'd helped Jack and Annie on the summer solstice by magically turning them all into seals.

Jack was stunned. He had never imagined that their two friends from Camelot might someday visit Frog Creek! "What are you guys doing here?" he shouted.

"Climb up and we will tell you!" said Teddy.

Jack and Annie hurried up the rope ladder. When they climbed inside the tree house, Annie threw her arms around Teddy and Kathleen. "I can't believe you came to visit us!" she said.

"It pleases me to see you, Annie," said Kathleen. "And you also, Jack." Her large blue eyes sparkled.

"It pleases me, too," Jack said shyly. He still thought Kathleen was the most beautiful girl he had ever seen. Even when she'd been a seal, she'd been lovely.

"We went looking for you!" said Teddy. "We climbed down and walked through the woods to a road."

"But the road was full of monsters!" said Kathleen. "A big red creature nearly ran over us! It made a honking sound!"

"Then before we knew it, a giant black monster charged at us! It had a ferocious growl!" said Teddy. "We came back here to gather our wits."

"Those weren't monsters!" said Annie, laughing. "They were just cars!"

"Cars?" said Teddy.

"Yeah, they have motors and people drive them," said Jack.

"Motors?" said Teddy.

"It's hard to explain," said Annie. "Just remember—in our world, you have to watch out for cars every time you cross a road."

"Indeed we will," said Teddy.

"Why have you come here?" asked Jack.

"We found a message for you in Merlin's chambers," said Teddy, "and decided to deliver it ourselves."

"So we climbed into the tree house outside Morgan's library," said Kathleen. "Teddy pointed to the words *Frog Creek* in the message and made a wish to come here. The next thing we knew, we were here in these woods."

Teddy pulled a small gray stone from his cloak. "And *this* is the message we brought you," he said.

Jack took the stone from Teddy.

The message was written in tiny handwriting. Jack read it aloud:

To Jack and Annie of Frog Creek:
My Staff of Strength has been stolen.
On the winter solstice, journey to the Land-Behind-the-Clouds. Travel toward the setting sun and retrieve my staff—or all will be lost.
Merlin

"Oh, wow," said Annie. "That sounds serious."

"Yeah," said Jack. "But why didn't Merlin send us the message himself?"

"We do not know," said Teddy. "Neither Merlin nor Morgan has been seen for days."

"Where did they go?" asked Annie.

"'Tis a mystery," said Teddy. "Last week I journeyed to the selkie cove to bring Kathleen to Camelot. She is going to be a helper in Morgan's library. But when we returned, we could not find Merlin or Morgan."

"We only found this message for you," said Kathleen.

"Aye, and I thought that when Merlin *does* return," said Teddy, "he will be greatly pleased to have his staff back. Much of his power comes from its ancient and mysterious magic."

"Wow," said Annie.

"In his message, he tells us to go to the Land-Behind-the-Clouds," said Jack. "Where's that?"

"'Tis a land far north of my cove," said Kathleen. "I have never journeyed there."

"Nor I," said Teddy. "But I have read about it in Morgan's books. 'Tis as bleak as a frozen white desert. I am eager to see it for myself."

"So you and Kathleen are coming with us?" said Annie.

"Indeed!" said Kathleen.

"Great!" said Jack and Annie together.

"If we all work together, we can do anything, aye?" said Teddy.

"Aye!" said Annie.

I hope so, thought Jack.

Annie pointed at the words *Land-Behind-the-Clouds* in Merlin's message. "Okay, ready?" she said to the others.

"Yes!" said Kathleen.

"I guess so," said Jack.

"Onward!" said Teddy.

"I wish we could all go there!" Annie said.

The tree house started to spin.

It spun faster and faster.

Then everything was still.

Absolutely still.

CHAPTER TWO

Land-Behind-the-Clouds

Jack felt the sharp bite of an icy wind. He looked out the window with the others. "Oh, man," he whispered.

The tree house was not in a tree—for there were no trees anywhere to be seen. Instead, it was sitting high on top of a steep snowdrift. Other drifts rose and fell across a vast snowy plain. Beyond the plain were hills and mountains.

"The books were right," said Teddy, his teeth chattering. "'Tis bleak here indeed."

"No, 'tis lovely," said Kathleen. "'Tis the land where the northern seal people live."

"Cool," said Annie.

Jack dug his hands into his pockets. He agreed with Teddy. The land did seem bleak—and freezing! "I wonder where Merlin's Staff of Strength is," he said, shivering.

"Let us begin our search!" said Kathleen. "The message tells us we must travel toward the setting sun."

Kathleen climbed out of the tree house window. She gathered her cloak around her and sat down on top of the snowdrift. Then she pushed off and slid down the steep slope.

"Oh, wow. Wait for me!" called Annie. She climbed out the window and followed Kathleen. Whooping, she slid to the bottom of the snowdrift. "Come on, you guys! It's fun!" she shouted.

Jack and Teddy looked at each other. "Shall we?" said Teddy. Jack nodded. He pulled his scarf tighter around his neck and followed Teddy out of the window.

Jack and Teddy sat down side by side. They pushed off and slid down the icy snowdrift. Jack couldn't help whooping, too. It *was* fun.

At the bottom of the drift, Jack and Teddy scrambled to their feet. Jack brushed the snow off his clothes. He could see his breath in the frigid air.

"It's j-just a little chilly," said Annie, hugging herself.

Only Kathleen seemed not to mind the cold. She was smiling as she lay on the ground, gazing up at the sky. *Her seal nature probably keeps her warm,* Jack thought with envy.

Teddy peered across the snowy plain. "I believe not one living creature is here but us," he said.

"Not true at all," said Kathleen. She pointed upward. "I see snow geese and whistling swans."

"I can almost see them, too," said Annie.

Kathleen stood up. She shielded her eyes and gazed across the plain. The cold sun was low in the sky. It cast long blue shadows beneath the snowdrifts. She pointed into the distance. "And see? A white hare is leaping home before dark," she said.

Jack looked where Kathleen pointed, but he couldn't see anything moving at all.

"I see a snowy owl, too," said Kathleen, "and—oh, no!"

"What?" said Annie.

"Wolves," Kathleen said with a shudder. "They just disappeared behind a snowdrift. My people greatly fear the wolves."

"You need not be afraid. I shall protect you," said Teddy. He took Kathleen's hand. "Come! Let us make haste toward the sun!"

Together, Teddy and Kathleen headed across the snow-covered plain. Their woolen cloaks waved behind them. Annie and Jack dug their hands in their pockets and quickly followed them toward the setting sun.

As Teddy, Kathleen, Jack, and Annie trudged across the frozen plain, the sun sank closer and closer to the horizon. Its last rays poured purple-pink light over the snow.

The wind blew against Jack's face. He looked down and kept walking. The cold felt like needles on his skin. Each icy breath was painful. He hoped they found Merlin's Staff of Strength soon. He couldn't imagine anyone surviving for long in this lonely, freezing land.

Jack's thoughts were interrupted when he heard Annie calling. He looked up. The sun had completely slipped behind the horizon. In the cold twilight, the snow had faded from purple-pink to a dark shade of blue.

"Jack! Come look!" Annie called. She, Teddy, and Kathleen were standing on the slope of a huge snowdrift.

Jack hurried to join them.

"Look!" said Annie.

"Oh, man," Jack said softly.

On the other side of the snowdrift was a glimmering palace made from huge blocks of ice.

Beneath the rising moon, its gleaming spires pierced the blue dusk.

"I wonder who lives there . . . ," said Jack.

"Let us go and find out!" said Teddy.

Teddy led the way down the slope to the ice palace. Long icicles hung like spears in front of the entrance.

"It seems no one has visited this place in quite a while," said Kathleen.

"Indeed," said Teddy. He broke off several icicles, and they clattered to the ground. "Onward?" he said.

The others nodded.

Kicking aside the chunks of ice, Teddy led them all into the ice palace.

CHAPTER THREE

The Ice Wizard

The air inside the palace was even colder than the air outside. Moonlight flooded through tall arches in the walls. The floor shined like a skating rink. Thick columns of sparkling ice held up a domed ceiling.

"WELCOME, JACK AND ANNIE," boomed a voice from beyond the columns.

Jack gasped. "Is that Merlin?" he whispered.

"It does not sound like Merlin," whispered Teddy.

"But how does he know our names?" whispered Annie.

"COME, JACK AND ANNIE. I HAVE BEEN WAITING FOR YOU," bellowed the voice.

"Maybe it *is* Merlin!" said Annie. "Maybe he's just using a different voice! Come on!"

"Annie, wait!" Jack called. But Annie had already disappeared into the sparkly room. "We have to follow her," he said to Teddy and Kathleen.

The three of them hurried after Annie. Beyond the columns, steps made of carved ice led up to a platform. Sitting on a throne on the platform was a huge bearded man.

The man on the throne was definitely *not* Merlin. He was dressed in a worn robe trimmed with dirty fur. He had a rugged, weather-beaten face, a bushy beard, and a black eye patch. He leaned forward and glared down at Annie with his one good eye.

"Who are *you*?" he demanded. "I was expecting Jack and Annie of Frog Creek."

Annie stepped toward the throne. "I am Annie and he's Jack," she said. "And these are our friends Teddy and Kathleen. We come in peace."

"Annie? Jack?" the man snorted. "You are not Annie and Jack! You are far too small!"

"We're not so small," said Annie. "I'm nine. Jack's ten."

"But you are *children,*" the man said with scorn. "Jack and Annie are heroes!"

"Well, I don't know if I'd call us heroes," said Annie. "But we sometimes help Merlin and Morgan le Fay."

"Annie, shhh!" said Jack. He didn't trust the man on the throne and worried that Annie was saying too much.

But Annie went on. "In fact, Merlin told us to come to the Land-Behind-the-Clouds today," she said. "He sent us a message written on a stone."

"Ah . . . ," said the man on the throne. "Perhaps you really are Jack and Annie." He leaned forward and spoke in a low voice:

To Jack and Annie of Frog Creek:

My Staff of Strength has been stolen. On the winter solstice, journey to the Land-Behind-the-Clouds. Travel toward the setting sun and retrieve my staff—or all will be lost.

Jack didn't understand. "How . . . ?"

"How do I know what was in Merlin's message?" the man said. "I know because I wrote it

myself! I hoped it would find its way to you somehow."

Jack stepped back. So Merlin hadn't sent them on this mission at all. The weird man on the throne had tricked them!

"Who are you?" demanded Teddy.

"I am the Ice Wizard," said the man. "The Wizard of Winter."

Teddy gulped.

Oh, no! thought Jack. They had heard about this wizard on their past Merlin missions. It was the Wizard of Winter who had put a spell on the Raven King and who had stolen the Sword of Light!

The wizard glanced coldly from Teddy to Kathleen. “And who are the two of you?”

“I am Teddy of Camelot,” said Teddy. “I am an apprentice to Morgan le Fay, in training to be a sorcerer myself.”

“A sorcerer?” said the wizard.

“Yes,” said Teddy. “My father was a sorcerer. My mother was a wood sprite.”

“And I am a selkie,” said Kathleen, “one of the ancient seal people.”

“So you are both from *my* world,” said the Ice Wizard. “You are of no use to me.” He looked back at Jack and Annie. “I am interested only in the two mortals, Jack and Annie of Frog Creek.”

"Why are you interested in us?" said Jack.

"Because of what you have done for Merlin!" bellowed the Ice Wizard. "For Merlin, you found the Water of Memory and Imagination! For Merlin, you found the Diamond of Destiny! For Merlin, you found the Sword of Light! Now I want you to find something for *me*."

"What do you want us to find?" asked Annie.

The Ice Wizard grabbed the black patch covering his left eye. He yanked it off, revealing a dark, empty socket underneath.

"Yikes," Annie said softly.

"I want you to find my eye," the Ice Wizard said.

"Oh, man," said Jack. He was horrified.

"Are—are you quite serious?" said Teddy. "You want them to find your *eye*?"

The wizard covered his empty eye socket with the patch again. "Yes," he said. "I want Jack and Annie to find my eye—and bring it back to me."

"But—why?" said Jack. "Even if we found it, we couldn't make it work. We're not medical experts or anything."

"And anyway, why can't you get your eye yourself?" said Annie. "You're a wizard!"

"DO NOT QUESTION MY ORDERS!" the wizard roared at her.

"Hey, don't yell at my sister!" said Jack.

The wizard raised a bushy eyebrow. "You are brother and sister?" he said.

"Yes," said Jack.

The wizard nodded slowly. His voice grew softer. "And you protect your sister," he said.

"We protect each other," said Jack.

"I see," whispered the wizard. Then his voice turned gruff again. "Long ago, I traded my eye for something I wanted very much. But I never got what I wanted. So now I want my eye back."

"Who did you trade with?" asked Annie.

"The Fates!" said the wizard. "I traded with the Fates! But they cheated me! And that is why I sent for you and Jack. You must go to the Fates and find my eye, and you must go alone."

"Why alone?" asked Jack.

"Because only mortals can undo a bargain with the Fates," said the Ice Wizard, "not wizards like me—nor seal girls, nor the sons of sorcerers, like your two friends."

"But Jack and I succeeded in our other missions because Teddy and Kathleen or Morgan and Merlin helped us," said Annie.

"What kind of help did they give you?" said the wizard.

"Well, mostly magic rhymes and riddles," said Annie.

"Ah. Then I shall do the same," said the wizard. He thought for a moment, then leaned forward on his throne. In a growly voice, he said:

Take my sleigh
And find your way
To the House of the Norns
In the curve of the bay.

Pay them whatever

They tell you to pay.

And bring back my eye

By break of day.

The wizard reached into the folds of his ragged robe and pulled out a thick string with a row of knots. "This wind-string will speed you on your journey," he said. He tossed the string to Jack.

What's a wind-string? Jack wondered. *And who are the Norns?*

Before Jack could ask any questions, the Ice Wizard pointed at him. "Now listen carefully to this warning," he said. "Beware the white wolves of the night. They may follow you on your quest. Never let them catch up with you. If they catch you, they will eat you!"

Jack felt a chill run down his spine.

The Ice Wizard picked up a carved wooden stick from the floor beside his throne. Its smooth, polished wood glowed in the moonlight.

Teddy gasped. "'Tis Merlin's Staff of Strength!" he said.

"Indeed," said the wizard. He turned to Jack and Annie. "Go now and find my eye," he said. "Or you will never see Merlin and Morgan le Fay again."

"What have you done with them?" cried Annie.

The wizard stared at her coldly. "I will not tell you," he said. "You will see them again *only* if you return my eye before the break of day."

"But—" said Annie.

"No more questions!" said the wizard. "Be on your way!" Before any of them could speak, the Ice Wizard slashed the air with Merlin's Staff of Strength and shouted a spell—"OW-NIGH!"

A flash of blue fire shot from the end of the staff. In an instant, Jack, Annie, Teddy, and Kathleen found themselves outside the palace in the freezing night.

CHAPTER FOUR

Take My Sleigh

Jack sat on the frozen ground. Annie, Teddy, and Kathleen sat nearby. They were all too shocked to speak. The night was quiet. Overhead the full moon shined brightly, and a few cold stars twinkled in the clear sky.

Finally Annie broke the silence. "I wonder what he did to Merlin and Morgan," she said.

"I wonder where you will find his eye," said Teddy.

"I wonder how we'll carry it around," said Jack.

"And I wonder if the wolves are near," said Kathleen. She stood up and looked around, pulling her cloak tightly around her.

"Well, does anyone remember the Ice Wizard's rhyme?" said Teddy.

"Yes," said Kathleen. She repeated the rhyme perfectly by heart:

Take my sleigh
And find your way
To the House of the Norns
In the curve of the bay.
Pay them whatever
They tell you to pay
And bring back my eye
By break of day.

"What are *Norns*?" asked Jack.

"I have read about the Norns in Morgan's books," said Teddy. "They are known as the Sisters of Fate. They spend their days weaving great tapestries. Their weaving determines the fate of all who live in the Land-Behind-the-Clouds."

"So the Norns have his eye?" said Jack. "That's who he meant when he said he 'traded with the Fates'?"

"It would seem so," said Teddy.

"He said we should take his sleigh to find them," said Annie. "Where's his sleigh?"

"Look," said Kathleen, pointing. "'Tis there."

"Oh, wow," said Annie.

Not far away, a strange-looking silver sleigh glided silently from behind a snowbank. The sleigh looked like a small sailing ship with shiny runners. No one was steering it, and no horses or reindeer were pulling it. From its mast, a white sail drooped in the still air.

As the sleigh slid to a stop, an eerie howl shattered the calm of the windless night.

"Wolves!" cried Teddy. "Let us make haste!"

Kathleen grabbed his arm. "Do not run," she said. "If we run, they will chase us."

"Yes, of course," said Teddy. "They must not see that we are afraid."

Another howl shattered the air.

"Run!" cried Teddy.

They all charged across the snow to the sleigh and scrambled into it. Jack and Kathleen stood at the front, and Annie and Teddy stood at the back.

"There they are!" cried Teddy, pointing. "The white wolves of the night!"

Jack turned and saw two large white wolves dashing across the plain in the moonlight. As the wolves ran toward the sleigh, their big paws scattered snow around them.

"Go, go, go!" Jack cried, clutching the front of the sleigh.

But the sleigh didn't move. And the wolves kept coming. "How can we make it go?" cried Jack.

"Use the wind-string!" said Teddy.

Jack pulled the knotted string the wizard had given him out of his pocket. "Use it *how*?" he shouted.

"Untie a knot!" said Teddy.

Jack pulled off his gloves. His fingers were trembling as he tried to untie one of the knots. *This is crazy!* he thought. *How can untying a knot in a string help us?* But soon he managed to loosen one of the knots.

A cold breeze began blowing from behind the sleigh. It ruffled the sail overhead.

"Untie another!" shouted Teddy. "Hurry!"

Jack quickly untied a second knot. The breeze grew stronger, and the sail filled out a bit more. The sleigh's shiny runners began sliding across the snow.

"Yay!" called Annie. "It works!"

"Yes, but not nearly swiftly enough!" said Teddy.

Jack looked back. The two white wolves had almost caught up with them. They were yelping and running behind the sleigh. Their mouths were open, showing their sharp teeth.

Jack quickly untied a third knot. A cold wind blasted the sail. It opened with a snap, and the sleigh shot forward!

"Stand fast!" cried Teddy.

Jack, Annie, and Kathleen held tightly to the sides of the sleigh to keep from falling out. Teddy grabbed the rudder and steered them over the snow, away from the ice palace.

The wizard's sleigh zoomed across the frozen ground, leaving the white wolves in its wake. Their yelping noises grew fainter and fainter, until they could be heard no more.

The wind kept pushing the silver sleigh over the ice and snow. The runners made *swish-swish* sounds as they slid over the moonlit plain. The square sail billowed in the wind, like the sail of a Viking ship. With the wolves far behind, the ride was really fun, but cold.

"How did you know untying knots would make the wind blow?" Jack asked Teddy.

"'Tis an ancient magic," said Teddy. "I have read of wind-strings but had never seen one."

"It's a good thing you read so much," said Annie.

"Oh, look!" said Kathleen. "Hares and foxes!"

"Where?" said Annie.

"There!" Kathleen pointed into the dark distance. "Playing in the snow! And listen! Whistling swans—overhead, behind that cloud."

"Wow," said Annie.

Jack was amazed by Kathleen's power to see and hear so many things. As before, the moonlit landscape seemed completely empty to him.

"Where are you steering us?" Annie asked Teddy.

"I have no idea!" said Teddy, laughing.

"We're supposed to go to a curve of a bay to find the Norns," said Annie.

"Then turn left and follow the swans!" said Kathleen, pointing across the snowy plain. "They are flying toward the sea!"

Teddy swerved the sleigh to the left. For a while, they bounced up and down over the snow. Then the ride grew smoother.

"We are on sea ice now!" said Kathleen. "Seals are beneath! I see their breathing holes! Perhaps we should stop."

"Indeed!" said Teddy as they whizzed along. "But how?"

"Try *tying* a knot!" said Annie.

"Excellent idea!" said Teddy. "Jack?"

Jack yanked off his gloves. With cold, shaky fingers, he tied a knot in the string. The wind lessened a bit. The sleigh began to slow down.

He tied another. The sail started to droop.

"Hooray!" said Annie.

Jack tied a third knot and the wind completely died away. The sleigh glided to a stop.

"Well done!" said Teddy.

"Thanks," said Jack. He tucked the string back in his pocket and looked around. "I wonder if this is where the Norns live."

"I will ask," said Kathleen.

Ask who? thought Jack.

Kathleen climbed out of the sleigh. She walked over the sea ice, studying it closely. Then she stopped above a small hole.

Kathleen knelt down and spoke softly in selkie language. Then she put her ear close to the hole in the ice and listened.

A moment later, she stood up. "The seal told me the curve of the bay lies just beyond those sea rocks," she said, pointing. "That is where we will find the Norns."

"Great," said Annie.

Jack, Annie, Teddy, and Kathleen crunched over the frozen sea under the bright moon. They walked through a narrow passage between the sea rocks. When they stepped out from the passage, they stopped.

"There 'tis," said Teddy.

About fifty yards away was a large, snowy white mound. Smoke was coming from a chimney on top of the mound. Lantern light flickered from a small, round window.

"I know you must bargain for the Ice Wizard's eye alone," said Teddy. "But I would at least like to take a peek at the Norns."

He moved quietly to the window and peered into the house. The others joined him. They saw a large fire burning on a hearth. In its rosy glow, three strange creatures were weaving at a big loom. Jack caught his breath. Their appearance was shocking.

The three Sisters of Fate were as skinny as skeletons. They all had straggly hair, long noses, and huge, bulging eyes. Their crooked, bony fingers fluttered over a large tapestry.

Around the room other tapestries were stacked to the ceiling.

"They look like witches in a fairy tale," whispered Annie.

"Aye, but they are not witches," said Teddy. "Every cloth they weave is the history of a life."

"Wow," said Annie.

"Well, good luck," said Teddy. "Kathleen and I will wait out here while you go inside and ask for the wizard's eye."

Suddenly a terrible howl pierced the silence.

"Yikes!" said Annie.

"The wolves!" said Kathleen.

Teddy hurried to the door and threw it open. "Everyone inside!" he said.

And all four of them scrambled into the House of the Norns.

CHAPTER FIVE

The Norns

Teddy slammed the door against the wolves. Jack caught his breath.

"Welcome!" the three Norns said in unison. They all looked exactly alike, except they wore gowns of different colors—blue, brown, and gray.

"How are you, Jack, Annie, Teddy, and Kathleen?" said the blue Norn.

"We're good *now*," said Annie.

Jack was amazed that the Norns knew all their names. Despite their strange appearance, their friendly smiles and twinkling eyes put him at ease. In their cozy house, he began to feel warm for the first time since they had left home.

"Was your journey pleasant?" asked the brown Norn.

"Yes. We came in the Ice Wizard's sleigh," said Annie.

"With the help of a wind-string," said Teddy. Jack held up the string to show them.

The gray Norn cackled. "Yes, we know! I like a string with knots," she said.

"A string without knots would be a boring string indeed!" said the blue Norn.

"A *life* without knots would be a boring life indeed!" chimed in the brown Norn.

As they spoke, the Norns kept weaving. Their bulging eyes never blinked. Jack sensed that they never closed their eyes—or stopped their work.

"Sorry to bother you," said Annie. "But Jack and I need the eye of the Ice Wizard of Winter so we can save our friends Merlin and Morgan."

"We know," said the blue Norn. "We are weaving the story of the Ice Wizard now. Come look."

Jack moved with the others to the loom. Dozens of tiny pictures were woven into the tapestry. The threads were all wintry colors—blues, grays, and browns.

"The pictures tell the story of the wizard's life," explained the brown Norn.

One picture showed two children playing together. Another showed a boy running after a swan. Another showed two white wolves—and another showed an eye in a circle.

"What's the story of the eye?" Jack asked.

"Long ago, the Ice Wizard came to us seeking all the wisdom of the world," said the gray Norn. "We said we would give him wisdom if he gave us one of his eyes. He agreed to the bargain."

"The wizard doesn't seem very wise," said Annie.

"Indeed he is not," said the brown Norn. "We planted the seeds of wisdom in his heart, but they never grew."

"Why did you want his eye?" asked Jack.

"We wished to give it to the Frost Giant," said the blue Norn.

"*The Frost Giant?*" said Teddy. "Who is the Frost Giant?"

"He is neither magician nor mortal," said the blue Norn. "He is a blind force of nature that spares nothing in his path."

"We hoped the Frost Giant would use the wizard's eye to *see* the beauty of the world, so he might choose to *care* for it rather than destroy it," said the brown Norn. "But alas, the Frost Giant does not use our gift at all! Instead, he keeps it hidden away—right where we left it!"

"Where's that?" asked Annie.

"The Frost Giant sleeps inside the Hollow Hill," said the gray Norn.

"In the Hollow Hill is a hole," said the blue Norn.

"In the hole is a hailstone," said the brown Norn.

"And in the heart of the hailstone hides the wizard's eye," said the gray Norn.

Jack closed his eyes and repeated:

In the Hollow Hill is a hole.

In the hole is a hailstone.

In the heart of the hailstone
Hides the wizard's eye.

"Yes!" said the gray Norn. "That is where you must go. But beware: *You must never look directly at the Frost Giant. Anyone who looks directly at the Frost Giant will freeze to death at once.*"

Jack shivered and nodded.

"Well, we'd better get going," said Annie. "Thanks for your help. The Ice Wizard's rhyme tells us to pay you whatever you ask us to pay."

The Norns looked at each other. "I like that weaving around her neck," the gray Norn said to her sisters. "'Tis red like the fiery dawn." The other two Norns nodded eagerly.

"My scarf?" said Annie. "Sure. Here." She took off her red woolen scarf and placed it on the floor near the Norns' loom.

"Lovely!" said the blue Norn. "Perhaps we will stop weaving fates and start weaving scarves!"

The other Norns cackled. "Well, go now," said the gray Norn. "Travel toward the North Star. When you reach the snowy hills, look for the one whose peak is missing."

Jack, Annie, and Teddy started toward the door, but Kathleen stayed behind. "Forgive me, but I have one more question," she said. She pointed to the picture of the swan and the boy on the tapestry. "What is this story?"

"'Tis a sad tale," said the gray Norn. "The Ice Wizard had a younger sister who loved him more than anything in the world. One day they fought over something foolish. He lost his temper and told her to leave him alone forever. She ran down to the sea in tears. There she found a flock of swan maidens. They gave her a white feathered dress. She put on the dress and became a swan maiden herself. She flew away with the others and never returned."

"After that the Ice Wizard was never the same," said the blue Norn. "When his sister left, he grew cold and mean-spirited. 'Twas as if his sister took his heart with her when she flew away."

"That *is* sad," said Annie. "How will the Ice Wizard's story end?"

"You—not we—will determine the threads we weave next," said the brown Norn.

"We will?" said Annie.

"Yes," said the gray Norn. "Our powers are fading. Our plans no longer work the way we expect them to. The Ice Wizard has no wisdom! The Frost Giant has no sight! *You* must go now and finish the story."

The three sisters smiled at their visitors. Their skinny fingers fluttered over their weaving like butterflies over flowers.

Jack couldn't help smiling back at them. But then he thought about Merlin and Morgan. He thought about all the dangers waiting outside. "One last question," he said. "What's the story of the two white wolves?"

"Oh, the wolves!" said the blue Norn. "Do

not fear the wolves! A life without wolves would be a boring life indeed!" Her two sisters smiled in agreement. For the moment, their smiles made Jack feel unafraid of the white wolves—and the Ice Wizard and the Frost Giant, too.

"Good-bye! Good-bye! Good-bye!" said the three sisters.

Jack and the others waved good-bye. Then they slipped out of the House of the Norns and into the icy night.

CHAPTER SIX

In the Hollow Hill

Standing in the cold, Jack felt afraid again. There were big paw prints in the moonlit snow all around the house.

"The wolves were here," said Kathleen.

"Perhaps we should go back inside," said Teddy.

"No," said Kathleen. "We must walk with Jack and Annie back to the sleigh and send them on their journey to the Hollow Hill."

"Yes, of course," said Teddy, nodding.

As they all headed cautiously toward the

rocks, Jack glanced back at the House of the Norns. He wished they could return to its cozy warmth.

Kathleen put her hand on his shoulder. "Come," she said. "You must hurry."

Jack trudged with the others through the passage in the rocks. When they got to the other side, there was no sign of the two white wolves. The silver sleigh was waiting in the moonlight. Jack and Annie climbed inside it.

"Can't you come with us?" Jack asked Teddy and Kathleen. "Remember you said if we all work together, we can do anything?"

"Aye," said Teddy. "But what the Ice Wizard said is true. Only mortals can undo a bargain with the Fates."

"Do not fear," said Kathleen. "We will be with you in spirit. And we will meet you back at the wizard's palace at dawn."

"How will you get there?" asked Annie.

"I have a few rhymes I can try," said Teddy, smiling.

"And I have a bit of selkie magic," said Kathleen.

"And we have our wind-string!" said Annie.

"Hasten, then, to the Hollow Hill," said Kathleen.

"And remember what the Norns told you," said Teddy. "*Never* look at the Frost Giant."

"I know," said Jack. He pulled out the wind-string. He took off his gloves and untied a knot. A breeze began to blow.

Jack untied a second knot. The breeze grew stronger, the sail unfurled, and the runners slid forward.

Jack untied a third knot. The wind blew hard. The white sail snapped, and the sleigh took off through the night.

"Stand fast!" Teddy called after them.

Jack and Annie waved good-bye to Teddy and Kathleen as the sleigh slid swiftly over the sea ice. Soon the sleigh bumped onto the snow-covered plain and veered off sharply to the right.

"No, toward the North Star!" Jack called to Annie.

Annie turned the rudder, steering the sleigh back on course. They sailed toward the bright star in the distance.

As the silver runners swished across the windswept snow, Jack braced himself against the cold. He kept a lookout for the white wolves, but he didn't see any sign of them as the sleigh sped across the moonlit plain.

Soon he could see a row of snow-covered hills in the distance. "Look!" he said. "There it is!" He pointed to one of the hills—the only one without a peak.

"Tie her down!" Annie shouted.

Jack tied a knot in the string, and the sleigh began to slow down. He tied a second, then a third. The wind died down completely, and the sleigh coasted to a stop at the foot of the Hollow Hill. Jack and Annie climbed out.

Jack looked up at the steep white slope. "How do we get inside?" he said.

"I don't know," said Annie. "How do you think the Frost Giant gets inside?"

"Oh . . . the Frost Giant," said Jack. He really wished Teddy and Kathleen were with them. He felt as if part of their team was missing.

Annie seemed to read his thoughts. "We can do it," she said. "We have to—for Morgan and Merlin."

Jack nodded. "You're right," he said. They studied the hill in the moonlight.

"Up there—is that an opening?" said Annie.

"Maybe," said Jack. "Let's climb up and check it out." When they climbed a little way up the hill, Jack could clearly see a break in the snow-covered slope.

"Let's see if it leads inside!" said Annie.

"Wait, what about the Frost Giant?" said Jack.

"I have a feeling he's not here right now," said Annie. "We'd better go in and find the wizard's eye before he comes back."

"Okay," said Jack. "But be careful!"

They scurried farther up the slope. When they came to the opening, they stepped through the huge crack into the hill.

Jack and Annie found themselves on a ledge above a deep, rounded hollow. Moonlight flooded down through the open hilltop. At the bottom of the hollow was a flat spot where it looked as if the snow had been blown in circles.

“That must be where the giant sleeps!” said Annie.

"Yeah, and it's probably where he hides the eye," said Jack. "We just have to find a hole. Remember?" He repeated what the Norns had said:

In the Hollow Hill is a hole.

In the hole is a hailstone.

In the heart of the hailstone

Hides the wizard's eye.

"Right," said Annie.

Jack looked down at the snowy swirl. He looked back at Annie. "Onward?"

"Onward," she whispered.

Jack and Annie scrambled down into the hollow. Stepping carefully through the silver moonlight, they studied the ground, looking for the hole.

Annie stumbled and fell. "Whoa!" she said. "I think I just found the hole! I stepped in it!"

"Really?" said Jack. He knelt down beside her.

Annie reached down into a small hole in the floor of the hollow. "There's something in here!"

she said. She pulled out a chunk of ice the size of an egg. "The hailstone!"

In the dim light, it was impossible to see if anything was inside the ice chunk. "We don't know if this is the right hailstone," said Jack. "We'll have to wait till daylight to see if the eye's in there."

"It has to be the right one," said Annie. "How many hailstones are hidden in a hole in a hollow hill?"

"Good point," said Jack.

Annie turned the hailstone over in her hand. "Maybe the eye is looking at us now," she said.

"That's scientifically impossible," said Jack. "An eye can't see unless it's connected to a brain."

"Yeah, and a string can't make the wind blow, either," said Annie. "Forget science in this place. Wait—" She caught her breath. "Did you feel that?"

"Feel what?" said Jack.

"The ground's shaking," said Annie.

Jack *did* feel the ground trembling. He heard

a strange sound, too—a loud huffing sound coming from outside the hill—*HUFFFF, HUFFFF, HUFFFF.* . . . It sounded like breathing!

"The giant's back!" said Annie.

"Oh, no!" cried Jack.

The ground kept rumbling. The breathing sounds got louder.

"Hide the hailstone!" said Jack.

Annie shoved the ice chunk into her pocket.

HUFFFF, HUFFFF, HUFFFF. . . . It sounded like the giant was entering the hollow!

"He's coming!" said Annie.

"Hide!" whispered Jack.

Jack pulled Annie into the shadows. He remembered the gray Norn's warning: *Anyone who looks directly at the Frost Giant will freeze to death at once.*

"Whatever you do, *don't look at him!*" he whispered to Annie.

Crouching in the dark, they buried their faces in their hands and waited. . . .

CHAPTER SEVEN

The Frost Giant

HUFFFF, HUFFFF, HUFFFFF. . . . With each breath from the Frost Giant, a blast of cold wind swept through the hollow.

Jack trembled. He felt chilled to the bone. *HUFFFF, HUFFFF, HUFFFFF*. . . .

The giant's breathing grew louder and stronger. Jack squeezed his eyes shut as icy, wet wind rushed against his body.

HUFFFF, HUFFFF, HUFFFFF. . . .

Jack crouched lower and held on tightly to Annie.

HUFFFF, HUFFFF, HUFFFFF. . . .

The giant's breath howled like a hundred ghosts through the hollow. Jack thought of the blue Norn's words: *He is a blind force of nature that spares nothing in his path. . . .*

But then the giant's breathing seemed to grow a bit softer. *What's happening?* Jack wondered.

The breathing grew softer and softer.

"Maybe he's going to sleep," Annie whispered.

The breathing became calm and steady. The wind died to a light breeze.

"I think the Frost Giant is sleeping," Annie whispered. "We should try to sneak out of here."

"Okay, but keep your eyes down. Just look at the ground!" whispered Jack.

"Right," whispered Annie.

Their heads bowed, Jack and Annie crept cautiously across the floor of the hollow and began climbing up toward the crack. Jack's teeth chattered, but he couldn't tell if it was from cold or fear.

Suddenly a deafening roar shook the night! The Frost Giant screamed with windy rage! He was awake!

Jack was blown to the ground. He tried to crawl across the snow, but he didn't know which way to go, and he was afraid to look up.

"Jack! This way!" Annie's voice called above the roar of the giant's breath. She helped him up and they struggled together against the wind. Finally they came to the crack in the wall.

Jack and Annie scrambled through the crack. Outside, the wild wind knocked them over, and they tumbled down the side of the hill.

The wind swirled the snow across the plain. "Annie! Annie!" Jack called. Where was she? Where was the sleigh? He couldn't see anything. He couldn't stay on his feet.

The wind roared even louder. An avalanche of snow came crashing down the hillside. When it hit the ground, the snow exploded into great clouds of white powder.

"Jack! Jack!"

Jack heard Annie's voice in the screaming wind. He tried to stand up. But snow kept falling on top of him, until he was completely covered.

As Jack lay buried under the snow, all his strength left his body. He knew he should dig his way out, but he was too cold and too tired. He was too tired to look for Annie. He was too tired to fight the Frost Giant. Instead, he closed his eyes and drifted into an icy sleep.

❄ ❄ ❄

Jack dreamed that cold fur was brushing against his face. He dreamed that a wolf was digging around him, nudging him, pushing him, sniffing him. . . .

Jack opened his eyes. He felt dazed. At first he couldn't see. But he could feel that he wasn't buried in snow anymore. He wiped off his glasses. He saw a low moon and some stars in a clear sky.

The Frost Giant must have left, Jack thought. But then he heard a panting noise. He sat up and looked around. One of the white wolves was crouching right behind him!

Jack scrambled to his feet. "Go away!" he shouted.

The wolf stepped back and growled.

"Go! Go! Go!" shouted Jack. He picked up handfuls of snow and threw them at the wolf.

The wolf backed away a few more feet. Jack looked around wildly. Annie was lying very still on top of the snow. The other white wolf was sniffing and pawing at her.

Jack's anger made him fearless. "Leave her alone!" he shouted. "Go away!" He scooped up more snow and threw it.

The wolf stepped back.

"GO! GO!" shouted Jack. "Get away! Leave us alone!" He glared angrily at the two white wolves.

The wolves stared back at Jack. Their yellow eyes gleamed.

"I'm not kidding—GO!" shouted Jack.

Jack stared fiercely at the wolves. Finally the wolves looked away. They glanced at each other and then slowly backed off. They looked at Jack and Annie one last time. Then they turned and trotted away over the snow.

Jack rushed to Annie. He knelt beside her and lifted her head. "Wake up! Wake up!" he said.

Annie opened her eyes.

"You okay?" Jack asked.

"Yes . . . I dreamed about white wolves," Annie murmured.

"Me too!" said Jack. "And then when I woke up, they were here! They were about to eat us!"

"Really?" Annie sat up and looked around.

"Yeah, but I scared them off," said Jack.

"What about the Frost Giant?" Annie said.

"He's gone, too," said Jack. "Come on. Let's get out of here!" Jack helped Annie up from the snow. "Do you still have the wizard's eye?"

Annie felt in her pocket. "Got it," she said.

"Good." Jack looked around. Beyond the

heaps of fallen snow, the silver sleigh was waiting for them. Overhead, the sky had turned to a light shade of gray.

"It's almost dawn," said Jack. "Remember what the wizard said? We have to bring back his eye by the break of day—or we'll never see Merlin or Morgan again!"

Jack held Annie's hand and they trudged together through the snow. When they got to the sleigh, they climbed inside. Annie took her place at the rudder. Jack pulled out the wind-string and untied a knot.

The breeze rocked the sleigh. Jack untied a second knot, and the sail began to fill. He untied a third, and the silver sleigh moved forward, gliding over the white ground.

Swish—swish—swish. The sleigh moved through the thick snow and away from the Hollow Hill. As they sailed over the white plain, the sky was turning from gray to pale pink.

"We have to go faster!" said Annie.

Jack untied a fourth knot. The wind whistled in his ears. The sleigh picked up speed. Annie steered it past the rocks and over the sea ice. She steered it over the plain, south to the palace of the Ice Wizard.

When the sleigh drew close to the palace, Jack tied a knot, and they began to slow down. He tied three more, and the sleigh came to a stop.

Jack and Annie looked around in the faint, cold light. "I wonder where Teddy and Kathleen are," said Annie. "They said they'd meet us here at dawn."

Jack studied the vast white plain, but he saw no sign of their friends. He wished he had Kathleen's vision. "I hope they're okay," he said. "I hope they didn't run into the white wolves."

"I have a feeling the wolves wouldn't hurt them," said Annie. "The wolf in my dream seemed nice."

"Dream wolves are different from real wolves," said Jack.

"I don't think we can wait for them," said

Annie. "The eye has to be back by the time the sun comes up."

"The eye!" said Jack. "We never looked to see if it was inside the hailstone."

Annie reached in her pocket and pulled out the hailstone. She held it up.

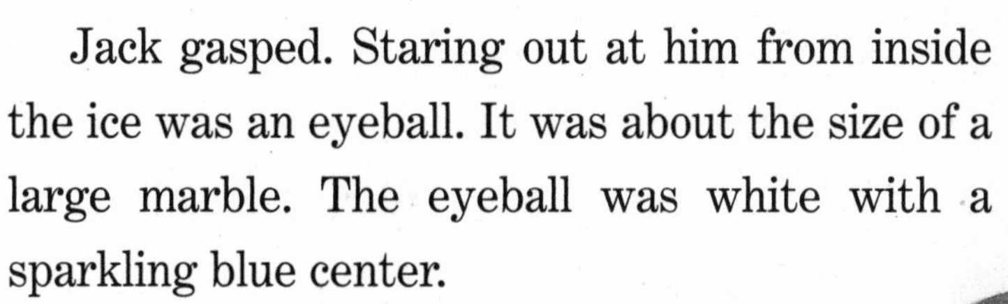

Jack gasped. Staring out at him from inside the ice was an eyeball. It was about the size of a large marble. The eyeball was white with a sparkling blue center.

"Oh, man," whispered Jack.

"It's beautiful, isn't it?" said Annie.

"I don't know about that." Jack felt a little queasy. Seeing an eye outside of a human head was too weird for him. "Put it away for now," he said.

Annie put the hailstone back in her pocket. Jack looked around again. The sky had brightened from pale pink to red. A thin sliver of the sun was peeking over the horizon.

"The sun!" cried Jack. "Hurry!" He and Annie jumped out of the sleigh and charged toward the palace.

When they got to the entrance, Annie stopped. "Look!" she said, pointing to big paw prints in the snow. "Wolf tracks!"

"Oh, no," said Jack. "Do you think the white wolves are inside? That's weird."

"It doesn't matter! We have to go in! Hurry!" said Annie. They rushed into the palace—just as the fiery ball of the sun rose over the horizon.

CHAPTER EIGHT

Return of the Eye

Jack and Annie walked through the front hall of the palace, past the ice columns, and into the wizard's throne room. The walls and floor glittered with the brilliant, cold light of dawn.

"Uh-oh," said Jack.

The wizard was waiting for them—and the two white wolves were sleeping on either side of his throne. Jack was confused. *Why are they here?* he wondered. *Do they belong to the wizard?*

The wolves lifted their heads and sniffed the air. Their ears pricked up. When they caught sight of Jack and Annie, they sprang to their feet. They stared at them with piercing yellow eyes.

The Ice Wizard was staring intently at Jack and Annie, too. "Well?" he said. "Did you bring back my eye?"

"Yes," said Jack.

Annie took the hailstone out of her pocket and held it up to the wizard. Jack watched the wolves nervously as the hailstone passed from Annie's small hand into the wizard's large, rough hand.

The wizard stared down at the chunk of ice. Then he looked at Jack and Annie. "Indeed, you *are* heroes," he said breathlessly.

"Not really," Jack murmured.

The wizard looked again at his eye inside the hailstone. Then, with a quick movement, he slammed the ice chunk against the arm of his throne.

Jack and Annie gasped and stepped back. The wizard slammed the hailstone against his throne again. This time, the ice cracked.

The wizard gently pried his eye out of the

heart of the hailstone. He lifted the frozen eyeball into the air and studied it in the light. Then, with an eager cry, he ripped off his eye patch.

Jack and Annie watched in amazement as the wizard fitted the eye into its dark, empty socket. Jack held his breath. He was horrified, yet fascinated. He couldn't imagine someone just shoving an eye back into his head.

The wizard slowly lowered his hand. He seemed to be holding his breath. He had two eyes. But the new one didn't move. It looked as if it was still frozen.

Jack grew worried. If the eye didn't work, the wizard might not help them. "We—we brought you your eye," he said. "So can you tell us where Merlin and Morgan are now?"

The wizard jerked his head to look at Jack. He covered one eye with his hand. Then he covered the other. In a frenzy, he went back and forth, covering and uncovering each eye.

Finally the wizard dropped his hand and

roared, "NO!" The wizard's howl shook the ice columns. "You have tricked me!"

"No we haven't," said Annie.

"This eye is useless!" cried the wizard. "It has no life! No sight!"

"But that's the eye you gave to the Norns,"

said Annie. "You promised if we brought it back, you'd give us Merlin and Morgan."

The two white wolves threw back their heads and howled.

"NO!" cried the wizard. "You tricked me! You tricked me!"

"Let's get out of here," whispered Jack. He pulled Annie toward the ice columns.

"STOP!" shouted the wizard. "YOU CAN-NOT ESCAPE ME!" He grabbed Merlin's Staff of Strength. The wolves growled and yelped. The wizard pointed the staff at Jack and Annie. He started to say a spell—"RO-EEE—"

"WAIT!" someone yelled. Teddy burst into the throne room. "Wait! Wait!"

The wizard held his staff in the air. He stared wildly at Teddy. His face was twisted with rage.

"We have something for you!" Teddy shouted at the wizard. "Kathleen!" he called.

Kathleen stepped out from behind the ice columns. With her was a young woman with long braids. The woman wore a flowing dress. Around her shoulders was a white feathered cloak. Her eyes rested on the wizard, and a radiant smile spread over her face. She began walking slowly toward the throne.

The wizard lowered Merlin's Staff of Strength. He stared back at the young woman. All the color drained from his face. For a long moment, he was as still as a statue. Then an ice-blue tear leaked out of his frozen eye and ran down his white cheek.

Jack and Annie stood with Kathleen and

Teddy. They all watched the young woman and the Ice Wizard gaze silently at each other.

"Is she his sister, the swan maiden?" whispered Annie.

"Yes," whispered Kathleen.

The swan maiden spoke to the Ice Wizard in a strange language—*"Val-ee-ven-o-wan."*

The wizard did not answer. Tears flowed gently now from both his eyes.

"Val-ee-ven-o-wan," the swan maiden said again.

"What's she saying?" Jack asked.

"She is saying, *I have come back to forgive you*," said Kathleen.

The wizard stood up. He walked down the steps from his throne. He gently touched the swan maiden's face, as if to make sure she was real. Then he answered her softly in the strange language. *"Fel-o-wan."*

"How did you find her?" Jack asked Teddy.

"A seal took us under the ice to the Isle of the Swans," said Teddy.

"When we found her, I told her how much the wizard has missed her," said Kathleen. "I also told her about the two of you and how you always help each other. I told her she should return to her brother and be his friend again."

The wizard and his sister kept speaking softly to each other in their strange language. Warm sunlight shimmered through the palace windows.

Annie stepped forward. "Um—excuse me," she said.

The wizard looked at her. "My sister has returned home," he said with wonder. "I can see with both eyes now. I can see perfectly."

"I'm glad," said Annie. "But now you must give Merlin and Morgan back to us."

The wizard looked at his sister. She nodded. The wizard held out Merlin's Staff of Strength. "Use this to bring them back," he said. "Hold it tightly and call out for them." He gave the staff to Annie.

Annie could barely lift it by herself. "Hold it with me, Jack," she said.

Jack stepped forward and grabbed the magic staff. The smooth, golden wood felt warm and vibrant in his hands.

As they gripped the staff together, Annie threw back her head and called out: "Merlin and Morgan, come back!"

A long burst of blue light shot out of the end of the staff—and flashed toward the two white wolves.

Suddenly wolf eyes changed into human eyes! Wolf noses changed into human noses! Wolf mouths changed into human mouths! Wolf ears into human ears! Wolf paws into human hands and feet! Wolf fur into long red cloaks!

The two white wolves were gone, and a man and a woman stood in their places.

CHAPTER NINE

Wisdom of the Heart

"Merlin! Morgan!" shouted Annie.

Teddy and Kathleen cried out in amazement.

Annie rushed to Morgan and hugged her.

Jack was filled with giddy relief. "Hi!" he said. "Hi!"

"Welcome back, sir!" Teddy said to Merlin.

"Thank you," said Merlin. He looked at Jack and Annie. "And thank you for turning us back into ourselves."

"We didn't know you and Morgan were the wolves!" Annie said.

"We were following you so we could help you," said Morgan.

"The wizard told us that if you caught up with us, you would eat us!" said Jack.

"Really?" said Morgan.

They all looked at the Ice Wizard. Standing with his sister, he stared guiltily at Morgan and Merlin.

"I feared that if they got close to you, they might discover who you were," he said. "But I will do no more harm, I promise—for I can see clearly now." The wizard looked back at his sister, and his blue eyes shined with joy.

"You can see because you have your heart back," said Morgan. "It was not only your eye that was missing—it was also your heart. We see with our hearts as well as our eyes."

"And now perhaps you can find the wisdom you were seeking from the Norns," said Merlin, "for wisdom is knowledge learned with the heart as well as the head."

The Ice Wizard nodded. "Please find it in *your* hearts to forgive me," he said. "Use my sleigh to take you safely home."

"Yes, indeed, we must leave now," said Morgan. "We have been gone from Camelot too long."

"The next time you come to Camelot, my friend, you must come as a guest," said Merlin, "not as a thief in the night."

"And you must bring your sister also," Morgan said to the wizard.

"Indeed I will," the wizard said.

Merlin looked at Jack, Annie, Teddy, and Kathleen. "Is everyone ready to leave now?" he asked.

"Yes, sir," they all answered together.

Merlin looked at the Staff of Strength in Jack's hands.

"Oh! Sorry, I almost forgot," said Jack. He handed the heavy staff to Merlin.

As soon as Merlin held the Staff of Strength, he seemed more powerful. "Let us be off!" he said briskly.

Merlin and Morgan led the way out of the throne room, their red cloaks billowing behind them. Teddy and Kathleen followed, and Jack and Annie hurried after them.

Just before they left the room, Jack and Annie glanced back at the Ice Wizard and his swan sister. They were deep in conversation again.

"They haven't seen each other for years," said Annie. "They must have a lot to talk about."

"Yeah," said Jack. He couldn't imagine not seeing Annie for years. "Come on, let's go." He took her hand and pulled her out of the throne room, through the front hall, and into the cold dawn.

Jack and Annie followed their four Camelot friends to the wizard's sleigh. Everyone climbed in.

Annie sat at the rudder. Jack stood at the front. He pulled out the wind-string and untied a knot. The sleigh rocked forward. He untied another, and the sleigh started moving very slowly.

The sleigh was heavier than before, so Jack quickly untied two more knots. The sleigh bolted across the snow.

"Stand fast!" said Teddy.

As the sleigh swished through the dawn, Annie turned to Morgan and Merlin. "I have a question," she said. "Can you tell us what the giant looks like—the Frost Giant?"

Merlin smiled. "There is no Frost Giant," he said.

"*What?*" said Kathleen and Teddy.

"Sure there is," said Annie. "We heard his breathing!"

"He nearly froze us to death!" said Jack.

"At night, the wind often swirls through the Hollow Hill like a cyclone," said Merlin. "You experienced one of those storms."

"But what about the Norns' story of giving the wizard's eye to the Frost Giant as a gift?" said Jack.

"Many ancient peoples believe that the forces

of nature are actual giants or monsters," said Morgan. "The Norns are the last of their kind. They hold to the idea that the Frost Giant is a living creature who haunts the Hollow Hill. In truth, the Frost Giant never accepted their gift because there is no Frost Giant."

Jack shook his head. "We believed what the Norns believed. They told us we'd freeze to death if we looked directly at the Frost Giant."

"And we believed what the wizard told us, too," said Annie, "that the wolves would eat us if they caught up to us!"

"People often try to convince us that the world is scarier than it truly is," said Morgan.

Right now the world didn't seem at all scary to Jack. Everything was calm and bright. Soft, rose-colored light was breaking through the morning clouds.

"Today is the first day after the winter solstice," said Morgan. "Today the light starts to return. The days will grow longer."

Jack turned to look at the sun. He caught sight of the tree house sitting on top of a snowdrift, not far away.

Jack tied a knot in the wind-string. He tied three more, and the sleigh came to a stop at the foot of the snowdrift.

Merlin looked at them. "On the winter solstice, you showed great courage," he said. "You endured storms and terror and extraordinary cold. You reunited the Ice Wizard and the swan maiden. And perhaps most important, you retrieved my Staff of Strength. I thank you."

"Sure," Jack and Annie said modestly.

"You have done much for the kingdom of Camelot on your last four missions," said Merlin. "On your next adventure, you will have a mission back in your world—in real time, not in the time of myth and magicians."

"We will call for you again soon," said Morgan.

"Great!" said Annie.

Jack and Annie climbed out of the sleigh. They looked back at Teddy and Kathleen. "I hope you will help us with our next journey, too," said Annie.

Teddy smiled. "If we all work together, we can do anything, aye?" he said.

"Aye!" said Jack and Annie together. Then they turned and trudged up the snowdrift. At the top, they climbed into the window of the tree house. Once they were inside, they looked back.

The sleigh was gone.

"Bye," Annie said softly.

Jack picked up the small gray stone from the floor. He pointed at the words *Frog Creek* in the wizard's message. "I wish we could go there," he said.

The wind started to blow.

It blew harder and harder.

Then everything was still.

Absolutely still.

❄ ❄ ❄

Jack opened his eyes. They were back in the Frog Creek woods. No time at all had passed while they'd been gone. It was almost twilight. Snowflakes fell like tiny feathers outside the tree house window.

Annie shivered. "I'm cold," she said.

"Here—take my scarf," said Jack. He pulled off his scarf.

"No, you need it," said Annie.

"No, take it. I'll be okay." Jack put his scarf around Annie's neck. "What will you tell Mom when she asks about *your* scarf?" he asked.

"I'll just tell her the Sisters of Fate took it as payment for telling us how to find the eye of the Ice Wizard in a hole in the Hollow Hill," said Annie.

"Right," said Jack, laughing.

"We'd better get home before dark," said Annie. She started down the rope ladder. Jack followed her.

As they stepped onto the ground, Jack remembered the wind-string. "We forgot to give this back," he said. He reached into his pocket and pulled out the string. "I guess Merlin's magic took the sleigh back to Camelot."

Jack and Annie looked at the string for a moment. "Untie a knot," Annie whispered.

Jack took off his gloves and untied a knot. He held his breath and waited. Nothing happened. He gave Annie a little smile. "I guess in our world, it's just a piece of string," he said.

Jack put the string back in his pocket. He and Annie started walking over the snowy ground between the trees. As they walked, Jack looked for Teddy's and Kathleen's footprints. But they were completely gone.

Jack and Annie moved out of the woods and down their street. They saw Christmas tree lights sparkling in people's houses and candles shining in windows.

Their boots squeaked as they crossed their snow-covered yard. When they got to the stairs of the porch, Jack stopped. He stared in astonishment.

Annie's red woolen scarf was draped over the railing of the porch.

"I don't believe it!" said Jack.

"I do!" said Annie.

They hurried up the stairs and Annie grabbed her scarf. "Look!" she said.

She held up the scarf to show Jack. There

was a tiny picture woven into it: a picture of him and Annie and two white wolves.

Jack was speechless.

"Cool, huh?" said Annie. She gave Jack back his scarf. Then she tied her scarf around her neck. She tucked the part with the picture under her jacket collar.

The front door opened. A delicious smell wafted out from the house.

"Hi!" said their mom. "The cookies are ready. Come inside and get warm!"

A Note from the Author

Some time ago I wrote a book called *Favorite Norse Myths.* In that book, I retold the myths of the Viking people, who lived long ago in the icy, rugged lands of Scandinavia. While I was working on *Winter of the Ice Wizard,* several elements from the Norse myths inspired the plot of my story. For instance, the Norse myths tell about a god named Odin who traded his eye for all the wisdom of the world, and they tell about Frost Giants, who represent the most brutal forces of nature. There are also three sister goddesses known as the Norns who decide the future. (In Greek mythology, three sisters called the Fates determine the future.)

While doing further research on the old legends of Nordic lands, I came across the swan maidens, women who could turn into swans, as well as wind-ropes (or wind-strings). I found out that wizards sold ropes with knots of wind to seafarers to help their ships sail across the ocean. Wind-strings are also mentioned in Hans Christian Andersen's story "The Snow Queen." The reindeer in "The Snow Queen" says that he can "twist all the winds of the world together in a knot. If a seaman loosens one knot, then he has a good wind."

Winter of the Ice Wizard closes this quartet of Merlin Missions. On these four missions, Jack and Annie find magical treasures for Merlin: water from the Cauldron of Memory and Imagination, the Diamond of Destiny, the Sword of Light, and the Staff of Strength. These four things were inspired by the Four Hallows of Camelot, which, according to Irish legend, were the four most sacred gifts of the ancient Celtic people.

Blizzard of the Blue Moon

Dear Reader,

Finally Jack and Annie go to New York City, the place I called home for over twenty-five years. New York City is a larger-than-life place, filled with skyscrapers, taxis, subways, parks, museums, theaters, and busy, bustling streets. The city has all kinds of weather, too, from heat waves to raging snowstorms. I remember one particularly dramatic blizzard in 1996. The city came to a complete standstill as the wind howled and it snowed and snowed and snowed. When the storm finally ended, pale sunlight shone on all the white streets and sidewalks—and everyone went out to play. Kids made giant snowmen and dogs tunneled through the snowdrifts.

No matter what disasters it suffers, New York City always comes back. I hope you have a great adventure there with Jack and Annie.

Mary Pope Osborne

He stays, the Unicorn,

In captivity. . . .

Yet look again—

His horn is free,

Rising above

Chain, fence, and tree.

—Anne Morrow Lindbergh,

"The Unicorn in Captivity"

Prologue

One summer day, a mysterious tree house appeared in the woods. A brother and sister named Jack and Annie soon learned that the tree house was magic—it could take them to any time and any place in history. They also learned that the tree house belonged to Morgan le Fay, a magical librarian from the legendary realm of Camelot.

After Jack and Annie traveled on many adventures for Morgan, Merlin the magician began sending them on "Merlin Missions" in the tree house. With help from two young sorcerers named Teddy and Kathleen, Jack and Annie visited four mythical places and found valuable objects to help save Camelot.

For their next four Merlin Missions, Jack and Annie were told they must travel to *real* times and *real* places in history and prove to Merlin that they could use magic wisely. First they went on a mission to the city of Venice. Next they journeyed to the ancient city of Baghdad. On their most recent trip they visited the city of Paris in 1889. Now they are waiting to hear from Merlin again. . . .

CHAPTER ONE

The Last Unicorn

The November sky was gray with clouds. Jack sat reading in front of the living room fire.

"Who wants hot chocolate?" his dad called from the kitchen.

"Me, please!" said Jack.

The front door burst open, and with a gust of cold wind, Annie rushed inside. "Jack! Guess what!" she whispered. "It's back!"

"How do you know?" said Jack.

"I was walking home from the library"—Annie paused to catch her breath—"and I saw a flash in the sky above the woods. The last time that happened—"

Before she could finish the sentence, Jack jumped up. "Dad, Annie and I are going to go outside for a while!" he shouted. "Can the hot chocolate wait till we get back?"

"Sure, have fun!" their dad called from the kitchen.

"I have to get my pack," Jack said to Annie. "Meet you on the porch."

"Don't forget the rhyme book!" said Annie.

Annie slipped outside and Jack ran up to his room. He grabbed his backpack. He checked to make sure their book of magic rhymes was inside. *Good*, there it was.

Jack charged back downstairs. He pulled on his boots, put on his jacket, tied a scarf around his neck, grabbed his mittens, and headed out the door.

"Come on!" said Annie.

Jack could see his breath in the cold air. "Brrr," he said. "Let's hurry!"

Jack and Annie ran down the street and into the Frog Creek woods. They wove between the trees, their boots crunching through the fallen leaves.

Jack stopped. The magic tree house *was* back. High in a tall oak tree, it was silhouetted against the gray November sky. "You were right," he said to Annie. "Good work."

"Thanks," Annie said. She ran to the rope ladder and started up. Jack followed her.

When they climbed inside the tree house, Jack and Annie saw a book and a scroll of parchment paper lying on the floor. Annie picked up the scroll, unrolled it, and read aloud.

Dear Jack and Annie of Frog Creek,

I am sending you on one more mission to prove that you can use magic wisely. This poem will guide you.

—M.

The very last unicorn
Is now hidden well
By those who have put him
Under a spell.

Four centuries, four decades
From that afternoon,
At the end of November,
Before the blue moon,

He will wake once more
And be free to go home
If you call out his name:
Divine Flower of Rome.

You must coax him to stand
Once his name is spoken.

His chain will break
And the spell, too, be broken.

Then a young girl must love him
And show him the way,
Lest he be trapped forever
On public display.

If he loses this chance
To rise and depart,
All magic will fade
From his horn and his heart.

"A unicorn!" breathed Annie. "I love him already. *I'll* show him the way!"

"But this poem is really hard to understand," said Jack. "What kind of research book did Morgan send us?"

He picked up the book that had been left for them by Morgan le Fay, the librarian of Camelot. The cover showed a row of skyscrapers. The title was *New York City Guide Book, 1938.*

"New York City?" said Annie. "I love New

York City! Remember the great time we had there with Aunt Mallory?"

"Yeah, I love it, too," said Jack. "But why would there be a unicorn in New York City in 1938? A unicorn is an ancient fantasy creature. New York City's a real place, and 1938 is not even that long ago."

"You're right," said Annie. "It sounds like a hard mission. But don't forget we have Teddy and Kathleen's magic rhymes to help us."

"Yeah," said Jack. He pulled out the book

given to them by their friends Teddy and Kathleen, two young enchanters of Camelot. "The problem is, we can only use each rhyme once, and we've already used seven out of the ten."

"Which means we still have three left," said Annie. "What are they?"

"Pull a Cloud from the Sky," said Jack.

"Cool," said Annie.

"Yeah, it is," said Jack. "But I'm not sure it will be much use." He looked back at the book. *"Find a Treasure You Must Never Lose,"* he said.

"Hey, that's a really good one!" said Annie. "The unicorn's a treasure. So that rhyme could take care of our whole mission."

"But it only *partly* fits," said Jack. "You could call the unicorn a treasure. But once we find him, we *have* to lose him. He has to go back home."

"Oh, right . . . ," said Annie. "What else?"

"Your favorite," said Jack. *"Turn into Ducks."*

Annie laughed. "I can't wait to use that one!" she said.

"I hope we *never* use that one," said Jack. He didn't want to waddle around and quack like a duck. "These leftover rhymes don't seem very helpful to me."

"Well, let's just wait and see," said Annie. "But now . . ." She held up Morgan's research book and smiled.

Jack nodded. "New York City, here we come," he said. He pointed at the book's cover. "I wish we could go *there*!"

The wind started to blow.

The tree house started to spin.

It spun faster and faster.

Then everything was still.

Absolutely still.

CHAPTER TWO

Who Are They?

Snow blew into the tree house.

Jack and Annie wore wool coats, hats, and mittens. Jack's canvas backpack had turned into a leather briefcase with buckles and a shoulder strap. Jack and Annie looked out the window.

Below the tree house was a wide, snow-covered field that ended in a wall of evergreen trees. Beyond the trees was a city skyline.

"This is definitely New York," said Annie. "See the Empire State Building? Remember our visit to the top?" She pointed to a faraway

building that rose above the others. "This must be Central Park. I remember that big field."

"Yeah, I do, too," said Jack. "But we've landed in New York in 1938. It was different back then." He opened their research book and read from the introduction:

> **The city of New York is the largest city in the Western Hemisphere. It covers an area of 322 square miles.**

Jack closed the book. "Whoa. Even in 1938, New York was a huge city," he said. "This is going to be like looking for a needle in a haystack."

"I'll read our mission poem again," said Annie. She read the first verse aloud:

The very last unicorn
Is now hidden well
By those who have put him
Under a spell.

"Okay, so this unicorn was put under a spell," said Jack, "and he must be hidden somewhere in New York, or Merlin wouldn't have sent us here."

"Right," said Annie. She read the next verse:

Four centuries, four decades
From that afternoon,
At the end of November,
Before the blue moon,

"What's a blue moon?" asked Annie, looking up. "I've heard that expression before."

"It's when you have two full moons in the same month," said Jack. "It doesn't happen very often."

"Oh," said Annie. She read on:

He will wake once more
And be free to go home
If you call out his name:
Divine Flower of Rome.

"Wait, does that mean the unicorn's name is Divine Flower of Rome?" asked Jack.

"I guess," said Annie. She read on:

You must coax him to stand
Once his name is spoken.
His chain will break
And the spell, too, be broken.

Then a young girl must love him
And show him the way,
Lest he be trapped forever
On public display.

If he loses this chance
To rise and depart,
All magic will fade
From his horn and his heart.

"So *I'm* the young girl!" said Annie. "And I

have to help him get home, or his magic will fade away forever!"

"Right," said Jack. "Okay. Let's review: There's a unicorn on public display somewhere in New York City. He's under a spell. The spell runs out in late November before a blue moon. But he'll only wake up when someone calls his name, which is *Divine Flower of Rome.* Then a young girl—*you*—must love him and show him the way home."

"Great," said Annie. "Let's get started."

"Get started? *How?*" said Jack.

"Maybe we should talk to some New Yorkers," said Annie. "We can ask them if they know anything about a unicorn in New York City." She looked out the window. "There're some people in the park right now."

Jack looked out. Through the falling snow, he saw girls crossing the field carrying skates. He saw two people standing on top of a small hill. One wore a cape, and the other a long raincoat.

"If we start asking people about unicorns, they'll think we're crazy," said Jack.

"Who cares?" said Annie. "Maybe *someone* will at least know *something* that can help us. Let's go down." She started down the ladder.

Jack quickly packed up their books. He buckled his bag and followed her. When they stepped onto the ground, Jack and Annie looked around. The skaters were gone. The two people on the hill were gone, too.

"Where'd everybody go?" said Jack.

"I don't know. But we'll find someone else. Come on," said Annie.

Jack and Annie started across the wide field. The snow was falling fast and furiously. The wind blew harder.

"Look, a frozen pond," said Annie, pointing. "That must be where the skaters were coming from."

Wet snow stuck to Jack's glasses. He wiped them off so he could see. No one was skating on the pond now. Whirlwinds of powdery snow swirled over the ice.

"Keep going," said Jack.

They kept trudging through the snow.

"Hey, look! Remember that?" said Annie.

"What?" said Jack. He wiped the snow off his glasses again. He saw a merry-go-round. "Oh, yeah." On their trip to New York with their aunt Mallory, they'd taken a ride on it. But now the riderless painted horses looked sad and lonely.

“I feel like we’re the last living creatures in Central Park,” said Jack.

“Which way do we go now?” asked Annie. “Which way did we come from?”

It was hard to see anything in the white haze of the falling snow. The buildings bordering the park and the skyscrapers in the distance had disappeared.

"Let's see what our book says," said Jack. He unbuckled his leather briefcase and pulled out their research book. He found a picture of Central Park and read:

> **Central Park is a vast natural area in the middle of New York City. The park has thirty-two miles of winding footpaths and covers 840 acres of land. It has rock formations, woods, and many bodies of water. It also has—**

"Okay, okay, got it," said Annie. "It's a *big* park. Is there a map that shows where we are?"

Jack tried to read from the index, but the wind and snow made it impossible. He stuffed the book back into his briefcase. "Forget it," he said. "Let's just try to get out of the park."

Jack and Annie turned away from the lonely merry-go-round and walked across the snow. A gust of wind blew Jack's cap off. As he turned around to grab it, he saw a couple walking a short distance behind them.

The two people looked like teenagers. They were walking with their heads bowed against the wind. The girl wore a dark cape with a hood. The boy wore a hat and a tan raincoat with a belt.

"Hey, look—" Jack said to Annie. But at that moment, the wind shook the trees, and big clumps of snow fell from the branches. Jack and Annie ducked and covered their heads. When the wind died down, Jack looked around for the couple.

"They're gone now," he said.

"*Who's* gone?" said Annie. "Who did you see?"

"Two teenagers, I think," said Jack. "A boy and a girl. We saw them earlier from the tree house. I think they might be following us."

"Wait a second," said Annie. "Two teenagers? A boy and a girl? Following us? Who does that remind you of?"

A big smile crossed Jack's face. "Teddy and Kathleen?" he said.

"Think about it," said Annie. "On our last three missions, it seemed like Teddy and

Kathleen were always nearby, wearing disguises, ready to help us when we needed it."

"Right," said Jack. "We could sure use their help now." He turned around. "Hello!" he shouted.

"Hello!" Annie yelled.

But the wind answered them with a howl. More clumps of snow blew down on Jack and Annie.

"Let's get going," said Annie. "They'll find us sooner or later. They always do."

CHAPTER THREE

Lost in Central Park

Jack and Annie kept walking until they came to the ice pond again. "We've been here before," said Jack. "We're going in circles. How do we get out of the park?"

"We have to try to walk in a straight line," said Annie.

Annie and Jack struggled on. Jack kept looking back, trying to catch sight of Teddy and Kathleen again. But it was getting harder and harder to see anything. Wet snow kept sticking to his glasses. Snow had blown up the sleeves of his jacket, under his neck scarf, and into his mittens.

"Yikes!" said Annie. She grabbed Jack's arm. "Look!"

A huge wolf-like dog stood on a ledge above them, his mouth open.

"Whoa!" said Jack.

The dog didn't move. He stood perfectly still.

Annie laughed. "Oh, he's a statue!" she said. She ran to a plaque under the dog statue, brushed off the snow, and shouted to Jack. "His name is Balto! In 1925, he carried medicine six hundred miles through a blizzard in Alaska!"

"That's really great," said Jack. "But how do we get out of the park?"

"Well, if we follow this path, it's bound to lead somewhere," said Annie.

Jack followed Annie up a wide path. They walked and walked, passing a snow-covered out-door stage and a fountain with the statue of an angel. Raising her outspread wings, the angel seemed about to fly away.

"Which way now?" said Jack.

Two paths led away from the angel fountain: one to the right, one to the left. "I don't know," said Annie. "Pick one."

Jack headed to the left. Annie followed. They passed a frozen lake and walked over an arched bridge. Jack kept his eyes on the ground and walked and walked and walked. Every time he lifted his head, the snow felt like needles against his skin.

Jack tried to keep walking in a straight line, but the path they were following began twisting and turning like a maze. Different paths branched off, curving this way and that. Jack remembered information from their research book: *The park has thirty-two miles of winding footpaths.*

"We have *got* to get off these paths!" he shouted to Annie. "Or we'll be lost in Central Park forever!"

Annie didn't answer. "Annie!" Jack shielded his face from the cutting wind and looked back. He didn't see her.

Jack turned around and around, looking for Annie. But he couldn't see anything—the world was completely white.

"Annie!" he cried. Had she gone off on another path? Was she lost? "Annie!"

She could wander around in the storm for

hours! thought Jack. *She could freeze to death! I have to find her!*

Jack tried to stay calm. He took a few breaths. *A rhyme,* he thought. He couldn't remember which magic rhymes were left. He struggled to unbuckle his briefcase—his fingers felt frozen. He pulled out the book and hunched over it, trying to shelter it from the storm. He wiped his glasses off and read: *Turn into Ducks.* That wouldn't help. *Pull a Cloud from the Sky.* That would only make things worse. *Find a Treasure You Must Never Lose.*

Is Annie a treasure? Jack wondered. He'd always thought of a "treasure" as something super valuable, like gold or silver or rare jewels. But right now Annie seemed more valuable than any of those things. She seemed like the most valuable thing in the world. Jack found the rhyme and shouted:

Treasure forever must never be lost!
Um-motta cal, um-motta bost!

"Jack!"

Jack whirled around. Annie was standing right behind him. "There you are," she said. "I was afraid you got lost."

"*I* wasn't lost," said Jack. "*You* were lost." He slipped the rhyme book back into his briefcase.

"Not me, *you*," said Annie.

"Whatever," said Jack. "Just stay near me now." He took her hand and gripped it tightly. "Okay, let's figure out what to do."

"Wait, is that a castle over there?" said Annie.

"A *what*?" said Jack.

"A castle. Look!"

Peering through the storm, Jack saw a small castle sitting on top of a snowy hill. A light burned in a window.

"A castle in Central Park?" Jack said. "That's weird."

"Let's go see if anyone's inside," said Annie. "Maybe they can help us. People in a castle might know about unicorns."

“Or at least know how to get out of the park,” said Jack.

Jack and Annie struggled up the stone steps that led to the castle. At the top of the steps, Jack glanced back at the park. He could barely make out two figures in the snow: one in a dark cape and one in a raincoat.

"Them—it's them!" said Jack.

A cloud of wind-driven snow blew over the couple. Jack kept looking, eager for another glimpse of the two young enchanters. But the snow hid everything in sight.

"They'll find us," said Annie. "Come on." She pushed open the door to the castle and led the way inside.

The door slammed shut behind them. Jack and Annie stood in a dimly lit hallway.

"Hello? Who's there?" a man called.

"Jack and Annie!" shouted Annie.

A tall, thin man came down a curving stone stairway. He wore an old-fashioned blue-striped suit. "Goodness! Two children!" he said. "What are you doing here on a day like today?"

"We got lost in the park," said Jack. "My

name's Jack and this is my sister, Annie."

"Pleased to meet you. I'm Bill Perkins," said the man. "Welcome to Belvedere Castle."

"What *is* this place?" asked Annie.

"The castle was built in 1869," said Mr. Perkins. "It was meant to be a delightful surprise when one wandered the park. Today it's a delightful surprise with a nature observatory and weather instruments inside."

"Weather instruments?" said Jack.

"Yes. I've come from the U.S. Weather Bureau to check them," said Mr. Perkins. "I'm afraid right now our data is telling us that the weather's undergoing a rapid and terrible change."

Jack shivered in his damp clothes. "Our data is telling us the same thing," he said.

"A storm has blown in from the Midwest, bringing wind and snow," said Mr. Perkins. "But after nightfall, things will get worse. Another storm is coming up from the South, gathering speed on its way."

“That sounds serious,” said Annie.

“It’s worse than serious,” Mr. Perkins said. “It’s disastrous. After dark, the two systems will meet and create a monster blizzard! It could be the worst in New York history! Even worse than the Blizzard of ’88!”

Jack caught his breath.

“Poor New York,” said Annie.

“Ah, yes, it’s the last thing our great city needs during these hard times,” said Mr. Perkins, shaking his head.

“Excuse me, but I have a question,” said Annie. “Do you know if there’s a full moon tonight?”

“Well, yes, there is,” said Bill Perkins. “You won’t see it, though—not through those storm clouds. Actually, it’ll be the second full moon this month.”

“A blue moon!” said Annie.

“You’re exactly right, a blue moon indeed,” said Mr. Perkins.

“I have another question,” said Annie. “Do you know where we can find—”

"Um—any unusual animals?" Jack interrupted. "On public display somewhere? In New York City?"

"Well, your best bet in New York would be the Bronx Zoo," said Mr. Perkins. "They display all kinds of animals from all over the world."

"Great!" said Annie. "How do we get there?"

"What? You can't go to the zoo today!" said Mr. Perkins. "Not in this storm!"

"No, no, of course not," Jack said quickly. "But if we ever decide to go to the zoo—in the future—how would we get there?"

"Well, the best way would be to take the West Side IRT," said Mr. Perkins.

"What's that?" said Jack.

"A subway line that runs up the West Side," said Mr. Perkins. "The number two train on that line will take you to the Bronx Zoo."

"Oh, great, thanks for everything," said Jack. "We'd better get going now." He and Annie started toward the door.

"Wait, there's a telephone upstairs. Let me

ring up your parents. Perhaps they can come get you," said Mr. Perkins.

"Um, well," said Annie. "We—uh—we haven't lived here very long, and we don't have a telephone yet."

"She's right," said Jack. "But it's not far to where we live. We just need to get out of the park to the street."

"To the West Side!" said Annie.

"Yeah, yeah, the West Side," said Jack. "Can you tell us how to get there from here?"

"Certainly!" Mr. Perkins opened the door. Wind and snow blasted inside as he pointed to the right. "Cross the terrace and then walk down the stairs to a path. That path will take you out of the park to Eighty-first Street," he said. "Hurry home now!"

"We will!" said Jack.

"Thanks a lot, Mr. Perkins!" said Annie. And she and Jack headed back out into the blizzard.

CHAPTER FOUR

Hard Times

The wind lashed the bare trees and swept the snow into tall drifts. "That way!" said Annie. She led the way down the castle steps to the path.

"Mr. Perkins was a nice guy," said Annie as they headed toward the west side of the park.

"Yeah," said Jack. "Someday I'd like to go back there and see all his weather instruments."

Jack and Annie trudged through the storm, until they saw buildings just beyond the trees.

"We're almost out of Central Park!" Annie said.

Jack looked around. "Do you see Teddy and Kathleen?" he said.

"No, but we'd better keep going if we want to get to the zoo today," said Annie.

Jack agreed. Mr. Perkins had said that the blizzard was going to turn into a monster after dark. And dark came early in November.

They left the park and came to a wide city street. All sorts of things were blowing about in the wind: newspapers, hats, and umbrellas turned inside out. Jack and Annie grabbed a lamppost and clung to it, trying to keep from getting blown away, too. When there was a lull in the storm, they trudged across the avenue. It was lined with cars half buried in the snow.

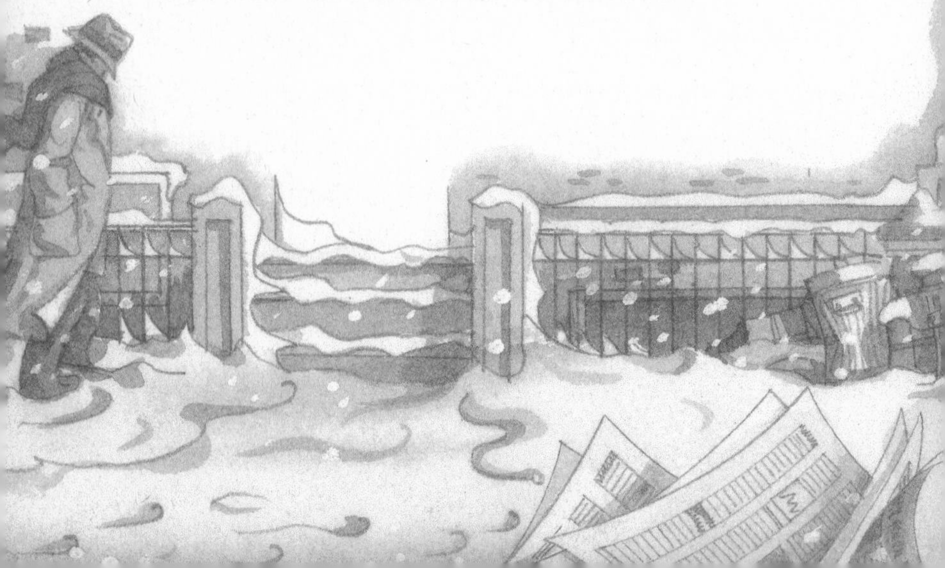

Jack and Annie started down a side street. They passed an old man and woman huddled in a doorway, wrapped in torn blankets, burning a fire in a small stove. They passed a line of men dressed in ragged clothes standing outside a building. A sign said "Free Soup."

Jack hoped everyone outside would find better shelter before the monster blizzard hit.

"Excuse me!" Annie called to the men in the line for free soup. "Do you know where the West Side IRT subway is?"

"Two blocks!" said a man. "Keep going!"

"Thanks!" said Annie.

Jack and Annie kept going. They passed a firehouse, a cheese store, and a newsstand. Everything was closed and shuttered. Peddlers' carts were stuck in drifts.

Signs banged in the wind. One said:

MEATBALLS AND BEANS—10 CENTS!

Another said:

ZITO'S BAKERY—5 CENTS A LOAF!

A third said:

LODGING—2 DOLLARS A WEEK!

Jack and Annie crossed the street. They saw newsboys huddled under a theater awning. The boys had wrapped their feet and legs in newspapers to keep warm.

"Excuse me, where's the subway?" Jack shouted.

"End of the block and around the corner! Green ball!" said a boy.

Green ball? wondered Jack. *What does that mean?*

"Thanks!" said Annie. "You guys should go home! After dark, the storm's turning into a monster!"

Jack and Annie trudged on. When they turned the corner, Annie shouted, "Look! A green ball!"

On top of a post was a large green ball. The post was next to a stairway that led underground. A sign said:

UPTOWN IRT TRAINS, 1, 2, 3

"That's it! Mr. Perkins said we take the number two!" said Annie.

"Wait, do you see Teddy and Kathleen?" said Jack, peering through the snow. Annie looked with him down the city street.

"I don't see them. But I'm sure they'll find

us," said Annie. She and Jack started down the stairs that led underground. The stairway was filled with people trying to get out of the storm. Jack and Annie walked with the crowd into the subway station.

A long line waited in front of a turnstile. A sign over the turnstile said:

SUBWAY: 5¢

"Oops, do you have any money for the subway?" Annie asked Jack.

"Yeah, I think I left home with at least a dollar in change," said Jack. He reached into his pocket and pulled out two nickels.

"Cool," said Annie. She led the way to the line.

As they waited, Jack looked around the station. A banjo player played a silly tune, but no one smiled. A man in rags walked around, holding out a hat, begging for money. Jack took another nickel from his pocket and dropped it into the hat.

"Thank you, thank you. Bless you," said the beggar.

"Sure," said Jack.

As the beggar walked on, Jack looked at Annie. "Boy, just a little nickel made him so happy," he said.

"I know. Everyone seems really poor and desperate here," said Annie.

"I wonder why," said Jack. While the line moved slowly toward the turnstile, he pulled out their research book. He read aloud from the introduction:

> **In the 1930s, New York City, as well as the rest of the United States, suffered through hard times known as the Great Depression. Jobs were scarce, and many people had no money or homes.**

"That's what Mr. Perkins was talking about," said Jack. "Hard times."

"I wish we could help everyone," said Annie.

"Me too," said Jack.

"But right now our mission is to save a unicorn under a spell," said Annie.

Jack frowned. "Our mission sounds like a fairy tale from a make-believe world," he said. "Not the real world of the Great Depression."

"I know," said Annie. "Hey, it's almost our turn. What do we do?"

"Let's watch the person in front of us," said Jack.

Jack and Annie watched an old woman put her nickel in the slot of the turnstile, which led to the train platform. The woman pushed through and joined the crowd of people waiting for the train. Jack and Annie put their nickels into the slot and pushed through, too.

The platform was bitterly cold. People looked worried, as if they feared the subway train might never come. Jack felt worried, too, but mainly because their mission wasn't making any sense. They were trying to get to the zoo before the blue moon, *and* before a monster blizzard hit the city. But when they got to the zoo, what then?

"This is what I don't understand," Jack said to Annie. "The poem says the unicorn is on public display. But if that's true, why haven't we ever read about New York City once having a unicorn in a zoo? That would be major news."

"Yeah, but remember the poem says he's 'hidden well,' and he's 'under a spell,'" said Annie. "So maybe the spell makes him look like a regular animal. But when we get to the zoo and say his name, he'll come out of hiding and—and—"

"Reveal his true nature?" said Jack.

"Exactly!" said Annie.

"Okay . . . ," said Jack. "But how will we know what kind of animal to look for?"

A signal bell clanged. Lights appeared at the end of the tunnel. Jack and Annie moved with the crowd as it surged forward.

The subway train rumbled down the tracks. On the side of the train, Jack saw a big number 2. "That's us!" he said.

7
79 REET
7
DANGER

2

When the train stopped, everyone on the platform crammed inside. Jack and Annie were squashed into one of the first cars. All the seats were taken, so they had to stand in the aisle. They held on to a silver pole as more riders squeezed into the subway car and grabbed straps hanging overhead. Jack actually didn't mind the tight squeeze. He was anxious to thaw out from the cold.

"Look, Jack!" cried Annie. She pointed out a window of the subway car.

Jack peered out the window, just in time to see two people rush across the platform toward one of the rear cars. One was dressed in a dark cape, the other in a tan raincoat.

A bell sounded. The subway doors closed and the train started down the tracks.

"Yay! They're on the train!" exclaimed Annie.

"Cool," said Jack, grinning. "We'll see them when we get off."

"Hey, *where* do we get off?" said Annie.

"Oh, man, we forgot to ask!" said Jack. He turned to the lady next to them.

"Excuse me, where do we get off for the Bronx Zoo?" he asked her.

"Tremont Avenue," the woman said gruffly.

"Where's that?" asked Annie.

"There's a map," said the woman. She pointed to a map on the wall above a row of seated passengers.

Jack and Annie stared at all the colorful lines that showed the subway system. "Nothing here makes sense," said Jack.

"Do you need help?" the girl sitting under the map said. She wore a tattered purple shawl over her head and shoulders.

"Yes, please," said Annie. "Can you tell us where we get off for the Bronx Zoo?"

"It's much further north," said the girl. I'll let you know when we get to the right stop."

"Thanks," said Jack.

The train bumped and creaked along,

stopping every couple of minutes. Jack looked out the window and tried to read the name of each station, but sometimes the platforms were too crowded. He was glad the girl in the shawl had promised to help them.

Just when Jack was starting to feel warm and a little drowsy, the girl called out, "Your stop's next!"

"Thanks a lot!" said Annie. She and Jack squeezed through the crowd toward the doors. When the train stopped and the doors opened, Jack and Annie were practically pushed out onto the platform with the other people leaving.

The subway doors closed and the train moved on.

CHAPTER FIVE

The Cloisters

"Do you see Teddy and Kathleen?" asked Jack.

The crowd was swarming away from the subway platform toward different exits. Jack couldn't see anyone who looked like the two young enchanters.

"No," said Annie. "But if we figured out where to get off, I'm sure they did, too. Let's hurry and get to the zoo. We can meet up with them there."

Jack and Annie moved with the crowd. They passed a change booth on the way out of the station. "Wait, I'll ask where to go," said Annie. She waited in line and then leaned forward to talk to the man in the booth. "Do you know how to walk to the Bronx Zoo from here?" she said.

"*Walk* to the Bronx Zoo? Are you out of your mind?" said the man. "This isn't the stop for the Bronx Zoo! It's much further north."

"You mean we got out at the wrong stop?" said Annie.

"You did, but it doesn't matter," said the man. "You can't get there now, anyway. The tracks near the zoo are above ground. And I just got word they're buried in snow."

"Oh, no," said Jack.

"Lousy day for the zoo, anyway," said the man. "Next!"

Jack and Annie stepped away from the booth and walked out of the subway station. The side-walk was deserted. "Oh, man, that girl gave us the wrong information," said Jack.

"This is terrible," said Annie.

"No kidding," said Jack. He looked around, wondering what to do next.

AH-U-GA! AH-U-GA!

"What's that?" said Jack.

"It looks like a taxi." Annie pointed at a big yellow car with a checkerboard stripe and writing on the side. Its horn let out a loud squawk: *AH-U-GA! AH-U-GA!*

The driver stuck his head out the window. He wore a big furry cap that came down over his ears. "Need a taxi?" he called.

"Yes!" shouted Annie. "Come on, Jack! He can take us to the zoo!" Jack hurried after her through the snow.

The taxi driver stepped out of the cab and opened the back door. "Hop in!" he said. His cheerful voice was muffled through a plaid scarf that covered half his face.

"Thanks!" said Jack. He stepped onto a running board and then climbed inside.

The taxi was very roomy. Jack could stretch his legs out and not even touch the front seat. "Boy, lots more room in old cars than ours," he said to Annie.

"Yeah," said Annie. "And there's no seat belts."

"Oh, yeah," said Jack. "I guess old cars didn't have any. I hope this guy is a good driver."

The driver slid open a little window that separated the front seat from the back. "Where to?" he asked.

"Can you please take us to the Bronx Zoo?" said Annie.

"We're in a big hurry to get there," said Jack.

"Sure thing, kiddos," said the driver.

"Great," said Jack.

"Oh, how much will it cost?" asked Annie.

"About thirty cents," said the driver. "Can you afford it?"

"Sure thing, kiddo," said Annie.

The driver laughed and closed the window.

Then the taxi began moving through the snow.

"Everything's so cheap here," Annie said to Jack.

"To *us* it is," said Jack. "But it's the Great Depression. Lots of people don't even have a nickel."

The taxi slid over the icy road and bumped over the curb. "Whoa!" said Jack, slipping off the seat.

"Sorry, kiddos!" called the driver. He got the taxi back onto the street. Then he plowed on through the snow, swerving this way and that.

The ride seemed dangerous in the bad weather, but Jack didn't want to get out now. He stared nervously out the window. The streets were empty of people. All the stores were closed and shuttered. Snow was piling up on apartment stoops, fire escapes, and iron balconies. Many of the buildings were shabby and crumbling, with broken windows.

"Hard times," Annie said softly.

"Yep," said Jack. He took a deep breath.

The taxi climbed up a road lined with tall evergreen trees. Suddenly it skidded and came to a stop. The engine roared, but the taxi's wheels only spun in the snow.

"What's happening?" Jack wondered aloud. He tapped on the glass that separated them from the driver.

The driver slid the window open. "Too bad, kiddos, looks like I'm stuck," he said.

"Are we near the zoo?" asked Annie.

"It's still a long ways from here, I'm sorry to say," said the driver. "But this taxi's not going anywhere. I don't know what else to tell you."

"Oh. Well, thanks," said Annie. "How much do we owe you?"

"Forget it, kiddo," said the driver. "Good luck!"

"Good luck yourself, kiddo," said Annie. She opened the door, and she and Jack climbed out into the cold wind. The taxi motor kept running, but the wheels only spun in place, sending up sprays of dirty snow.

"I don't believe this," said Jack.

"Maybe there's a subway station somewhere near here," said Annie.

"The man in the booth said the subways aren't running all the way to the zoo," said Jack.

"I know, but maybe we can at least get closer," said Annie.

Jack and Annie struggled through the storm until they came to a steep cliff. Over the edge of the cliff they saw nothing but a cloud of wind-blown snow.

"Where are we?" said Annie.

"I have no idea," said Jack. His teeth chattered. His eyes and ears stung with the cold, and his hands and feet felt numb. *Isn't this what frostbite feels like?* he thought. *Numb?*

"Let's go back and sit in that taxi until we figure out what to do," said Jack. "At least get out of the wind."

"Okay," said Annie. "Maybe the driver will get it going again."

Jack and Annie headed back the way they'd come. But the taxi was gone!

"Hey, he must've got unstuck!" said Annie. "And he left us!"

"Oh, man," said Jack. "We're having really rotten luck. And I think I'm starting to get frostbite. Seriously."

"It looks like there's a building over there," said Annie. "I see a tower."

"Yeah, me too," said Jack. "Let's go there and try to figure out what to do next."

Jack and Annie trekked up what looked like a long driveway until they came to the gray stone building. Jack wiped snow from a sign in front.

CLOISTERS OF THE METROPOLITAN MUSEUM, OPEN TO THE PUBLIC

"A museum!" said Annie. "Let's go in and ask them how to get to the zoo."

"Yeah, and get warm for a minute," said Jack.

He and Annie climbed the snow-covered steps of the Cloisters. Annie opened the door, and the wind nearly swept them inside.

They pushed the door shut.

"Ah! My first visitors all day!" a woman chirped.

Jack and Annie turned around. A museum lady sat at a desk in a corner. Dressed in a green uniform, she was tall and thin with a friendly face and short gray hair.

"I'm sorry, but we can't stay long," said Annie. "We just came here to get warm for a minute and get some information."

"What can I tell you?" the woman asked.

"We're trying to get to the Bronx Zoo," said Jack. "Is there a subway near here?"

"Well, the A train is close by," said the museum lady. "But that won't take you anywhere near the zoo."

"Oh, darn," said Annie.

"Oh, I wouldn't be so sad," the woman said

brightly. "If I were you, I'd stay right here and enjoy the Cloisters! You won't regret it, I promise. The Cloisters holds most of the medieval collection of the world-famous Metropolitan Museum of Art."

"What's a cloister?" Annie asked.

"It's an enclosed garden or courtyard," said the museum lady. "We have four in all. They beautifully evoke medieval times, from the Romanesque period to the light, airy elegance of the Gothic."

"Cool," said Jack politely. He had no idea what she was talking about.

"I suppose the gardens *are* cool most days, my dear," said the woman. "But today they are freezing! Never mind, you don't have to spend time in the gardens to enjoy the museum. Inside, we have many beautiful exhibits. The tapestries are especially lovely. They were woven with beautiful yarns by weavers from the Netherlands. For years, they hung in a French castle and managed to escape destruction during the Revolution. Then, for two generations—"

"Excuse me," said Jack. He was eager to end the woman's boring lecture so they could be on their way.

But she kept talking excitedly. "The tapestries were used by peasants to protect potatoes stored in their barns until, eventually, a countess rescued them. They were restored, and in 1922, Mr. John D. Rockefeller bought them. Just last year, Mr. Rockefeller gave them as gifts to—"

"Oh, that is so cool!" interrupted Jack loudly. He pretended to be interested so they could escape. "We'd *love* to see them! Where are they?"

"The tapestry room is just on the other side of the first cloister," the woman said, pointing. "Turn that corner, go out the door, and then walk through the garden to the door of the tapestry room."

"Let's go, Annie. Quick!" said Jack. He and Annie went around the corner, out the door, and into a snowy garden.

“Whew!” said Jack. “I didn’t want to be rude. But we’re short on time.”

“I know,” said Annie.

"What now?" said Jack, shivering in the cold.

"We need to figure out exactly where we are," said Annie, "and where the Bronx Zoo is. Maybe we can just walk there from here."

"Come on, let's get inside the tapestry room and check our research book for a map," said Jack.

They walked along the edge of the garden under a covered walkway. When they came to a door, Jack pushed it open, and he and Annie slipped out of the cold into a large, warm room.

Jack closed the door against the storm and unbuckled his briefcase to take out their research book.

"Ohh . . . wow!" breathed Annie.

"What? What?" said Jack. He looked up.

The walls of the room were covered with cloth hangings—tapestries shimmering with gold and silver.

"Oh . . . !" whispered Jack.

"A *unicorn*!" said Annie.

CHAPTER SIX

The Hunt of the Unicorn

There were seven tapestries in all. Each was almost as high as the wooden ceiling. Jack read aloud from a sign on the wall under the first one:

> ***The Hunt of the Unicorn***
> **Tapestries woven in the Netherlands**
> **at the end of the 1400s**

The first tapestry showed hunters and hounds searching for the unicorn. The second showed the unicorn being found.

The other tapestries showed the unicorn trying to escape, leaping from a stream, chased by hounds, then captured and slain by the hunters' spears.

Oddly, the last tapestry showed the unicorn alive again. He was sitting in a garden of flowers surrounded by a wooden fence. There was a wide blue and gold collar around his neck, and he was chained to a tree.

"That's *him,*" Annie said softly.

"How can it be him?" said Jack. "He's a picture in a tapestry."

"Read Merlin's poem again," said Annie.

Jack unbuckled his briefcase and pulled out the parchment scroll. He read aloud.

The very last unicorn
Is now hidden well
By those who have put him
Under a spell.

"The unicorn is hidden in the tapestry," said Annie. "The people who wove it must be the ones who put him under a spell."

"Hmm . . . ," said Jack. He read on.

Four centuries, four decades
From that afternoon,
At the end of November,
Before the blue moon . . .

"Stop, do the math," said Annie.

"Right," said Jack. He took out his notebook and pencil. "Okay, four centuries is four hundred, and four decades is forty. Add 'em up, you get four hundred forty. Then if you subtract four hundred forty from 1938, you get . . . 1498."

"It works!" said Annie. "The sign says the tapestries were woven at the end of the 1400s! And it's the end of November, and Mr. Perkins said there's a blue moon tonight!"

"Oh, man," whispered Jack. He kept reading.

He will wake once more
And be free to go home
If you call out his name:
Divine Flower of Rome.

Annie looked up at the tapestry. "*Divine Flower!*" she called.

Nothing happened.

"Divine Flower of Rome!" Jack called.

Jack and Annie watched and waited. Nothing changed in the tapestry. It looked exactly the same.

"Maybe he's not the right unicorn after all," said Jack.

"Maybe it's just not the right name," said Annie. "Read the rest."

Jack read more of the poem.

You must coax him to stand
Once his name is spoken.
His chain will break
And the spell, too, be broken.

"He *is* the right unicorn!" said Annie. "See? There's the chain!" She pointed to the chain in the last tapestry.

"Yeah, but why didn't calling his name work?" said Jack. "Why didn't he wake up?"

"I don't know," said Annie. "What else does the poem say?"

Jack read on.

Then a young girl must love him
And show him the way,
Lest he be trapped forever
On public display.

If he loses this chance
To rise and depart,
All magic will fade
From his horn and his heart.

"He *is* on public display, and *I'm* the girl, Jack!" said Annie. "I love him a lot! I'll show him the way!"

"Okay, calm down. First we need to wake him up," said Jack.

Voices came from outside. Jack moved to a window. He looked out into the courtyard. Two people were coming through the cloister, their heads down against the flying snow. One wore a dark cape, and the other a tan raincoat.

Jack turned back to Annie, a big grin on his face. "You were right! They found us! Teddy and

Kathleen are here!" he said. "*They'll* know how to break the spell!"

"Of course!" said Annie, beaming. "Quick, let's hide and surprise *them* for a change."

"In there!" said Jack. He and Annie hurried into a long room off the tapestry room. They heard the door from the cloister open. They felt a rush of cold air. They heard footsteps.

Jack and Annie grinned at each other. Jack put his finger to his lips. Then a quick, nervous boy's voice came from the tapestry room: "Grinda, they are not here!"

"I see that, Balor, but *look*—"

"Ahh! Is it *him,* Grinda?"

Annie grabbed Jack's arm. "Balor? Grinda?" she whispered.

"Shh," whispered Jack.

"Of course 'tis him!" said the girl. "I told you those Frog Creek brats would lead us to him! Get the rope ready!"

"Aye," said the boy.

Jack and Annie carefully peeked around the

corner. They saw a girl and boy standing with their backs to them, facing the unicorn in the last tapestry. The boy held a thick black rope.

"Call out his name, Grinda," said the boy.

The girl took a step toward the tapestry. She raised her arms in front of the unicorn. "*Dianthus!*" she called.

Wind whistled through the open doorway. The flowers in the tapestry swayed as if the wind were blowing them. The scent of roses wafted through the room. The unicorn moved his head.

"Ohh!" whispered Annie.

"Get ready, Balor, to take him back to the Master," said the girl.

Annie clutched Jack's arm. "Who's the Master?" she whispered.

"I don't know," whispered Jack. "But I don't think he's a good guy."

The girl turned back to the tapestry and spoke softly to the unicorn. "Come, come, my lovely Dianthus, stand up now. Come out of that old rug. . . ."

The unicorn turned his head and looked out at the girl. The look in his blue eyes was ancient yet young, wise yet innocent. He lifted his head as if he were about to stand.

The girl nodded to the boy. The boy slowly coiled the black rope into a noose. The girl looked at the unicorn again. "Come to me, Dianthus!" she coaxed. "Don't be afraid. I'll love you and show you the way—"

"No, Dianthus!" yelled Annie. "Don't go to her!" Annie and Jack bolted from their hiding place.

Balor and Grinda whirled around in surprise. They both had pale faces and pale shining eyes.

"Leave him alone!" Annie yelled at the strange pair. "You don't love him! *We* love him!"

At that moment, there was a flash of light, and the unicorn in the tapestry leapt like a deer over the woven fence. Balor and Grinda shrieked and jumped back. Jack covered his head.

Then there was silence. Jack looked up. The tapestry on the wall was unchanged—it still showed a unicorn woven from yarn chained to a tree.

But standing on the floor of the museum was the most beautiful creature Jack had ever seen.

CHAPTER SEVEN

Dianthus

The unicorn had a broad milk-white chest and graceful neck. A tuft of hair curled under his chin. A long, spiraled horn rose from the middle of his forehead. He stood very still and very tall. His whole body seemed to be glowing.

Balor and Grinda just stared at him. They both looked frightened. But Annie stepped forward. "Hi, Dianthus," she whispered. She reached out and gently touched the unicorn's white chest. "Feel, Jack, feel his heart pounding."

"Move away!" ordered Grinda. The girl stepped

between Jack and Annie. "He is ours and he is coming with us."

"He's *not* yours!" said Annie.

"Who *are* you, anyway?" said Jack. "Where did you come from?"

Grinda glared at Jack. "We come from the same magic world *he* comes from," she said. "He belongs with us, not *you.* Balor!"

The boy shoved Annie aside and tried to loop the black rope around the unicorn's neck. But Dianthus reared up and wheeled around, forcing Balor and Grinda out of his way.

Dianthus leapt across the tapestry room toward the garden. Jack and Annie followed him through the open doorway into the snowy cloister. Balor and Grinda charged after them. They pushed past Jack and Annie to Dianthus. Balor grabbed the unicorn's blue collar. "You are coming with us, stupid, like it or not!"

"Don't pull on him!" yelled Annie. "And don't call him stupid!"

Dianthus tried to back up.

"Let go!" screamed Annie. "He doesn't want to go with you!"

"He has no choice," said Grinda. "As soon as that rope goes around his neck, all three of us will be instantly transported back to the Castle of the Dark Wizard."

"No!" Jack shouted. He charged at Balor and tried to grab the rope from his hand. Balor let go of the unicorn's collar and shoved Jack into the snow. Then he turned back to the unicorn and began to swing the magic rope like a lasso.

Dianthus reared up again and kicked his legs. Breath from his nostrils billowed into the icy air.

"A rhyme, Jack!" yelled Annie. "A rhyme!"

Kneeling in the snow, Jack yanked the book from his briefcase. He frantically turned the pages, looking for a rhyme they hadn't used. *"Call a Cloud from the Sky?"* he shouted to Annie.

"Anything!" she called. "Try it!"

Jack read the rhyme aloud:

Down from high, out of the sky,

Ee-no-fain-ee-ro-lie!

A thick white fog instantly filled the cloister. The fog was so dense that Jack couldn't even see his own hand.

"Balor, where are you?" shrieked Grinda.

"Here!" the boy yelled.

Someone grabbed Jack. He struggled to break free. "Let me go!" he shouted.

"It's me!" whispered Annie. "Come on!"

Jack stood up, clinging to Annie. They stumbled together through the garden. Feeling their way along the walkway, they came to the door that led to the main hall.

"Dianthus, here!" Annie whispered.

Jack heard the soft crunch of the unicorn's hooves in the frozen snow.

"Where did he go?" Balor shouted.

"Find him!" yelled Grinda.

Jack reached out and felt the unicorn's soft mane. Annie pushed open the door. Then she, Dianthus, and Jack slipped inside the main hall.

Jack closed the door before Balor and Grinda could escape the garden. There wasn't a wisp of fog in the main hall. The museum lady was still behind her desk. She stared at Jack, Annie, and the glowing unicorn that had just come in from the garden. Her mouth opened, and then closed.

Dianthus stepped lightly over the wooden floor. Jack and Annie followed him.

The museum lady never blinked. As Dianthus walked gracefully past her desk, she reached out and touched him. She gasped and quickly drew back her hand.

"Thanks for keeping the museum open today," said Annie. "And thank Mr. Rockefeller for his gifts."

The museum lady opened and closed her mouth again, still unable to speak.

Jack opened the door that led to the street. Jack and Annie followed Dianthus out of the museum and down the stone steps. The blizzard had gotten much worse. Snow was coming down harder than ever. The wind was wailing. The unicorn shook his head and knelt down.

"He wants us to get on his back!" said Annie. "Quick! Climb on behind me!" Annie climbed onto the unicorn's back. Jack climbed on behind her.

Dianthus stood up to his full height.

Grinda and Balor burst out the door of the museum. "Stop!" screamed Grinda.

Dianthus looked back at them. Then he leapt nimbly over a snowdrift and headed into the darkening storm.

CHAPTER EIGHT

Back to Life

Jack clung to Annie. Dianthus cleared the driveway of the Cloisters and began to run with ease down the street. His long strides were so light and graceful, Jack could hardly feel the movement.

As the unicorn ran, he held his head high. His long, spiraled horn pierced the raging storm, seeming to calm the winds and snow. Jack realized he could feel his fingers and toes again. His whole body began to feel warm.

Dianthus headed down a deserted parkway along the waterfront, past an empty bridge. The bridge's towers and cables formed a silver arc over a wide river. Whitecaps swept across the water's surface. As the unicorn trotted past the river, the water became still.

Dianthus left the riverside and headed down a city street. The wind whistled between tall buildings, blowing the snow into great drifts. But the unicorn's horn turned the howling wind into a soft breeze. The wild blowing snow became floating, star-shaped flakes, like the snowflakes on Christmas cards.

As the unicorn trotted down the street, snowbound taxis and streetcars started moving again. Lights came on in cafés and jazz clubs. Jack heard happy music coming from inside.

With a calm, steady trot, the unicorn pranced on through the city. As he moved past old mansions, broken-down tenements, and shabby hotels, people peeked out of doorways and windows to see why the sounds of the storm had died away. When they caught sight of Dianthus, with his horn shining in the windless air, they broke into joyful smiles. Church bells started ringing through the white silence.

Finally Dianthus came to a stone wall bordering Central Park. He jumped over the wall and landed knee-deep in a heap of snow. The unicorn leapt effortlessly out of the drift and cantered over a field and down a slope.

Slowly the clouds parted, and light from the setting sun poured down.

"Hot corn!" a peddler shouted, plowing his pushcart through the snow.

"Roasted chestnuts!" shouted another.

The good smells of the corn and nuts filled the

CHOP SUEY
JAZZ

crisp golden air of the park. The unicorn trotted past Belvedere Castle. Bill Perkins stood outside, staring up at the clear blue sky.

"Hey, Mr. Perkins, the monster storm's not coming!" shouted Annie.

The weatherman saw Jack and Annie on the back of the white unicorn. His jaw dropped. Then he smiled and waved.

Jack and Annie rode on. When they passed the statue of the winged angel, Jack thought he saw her move her great wings. "Did you see that?" he cried.

"Yes!" said Annie.

When they passed the statue of Balto, Jack heard the sled dog bark.

When they rode past the merry-go-round, Jack heard a chorus of neighs and whinnies accompanied by lively carousel music.

Dianthus pranced down a shimmering pathway. He leapt over a stone wall and cantered over another field.

The unicorn's horn glistened, and the snowy field reflected gold and copper light. Not until the unicorn came to the tree that held the tree house did he stop.

Annie hugged the unicorn's long, graceful neck. "Thank you, thank you!" she whispered, and kissed him.

"Yeah, wow," breathed Jack.

Annie looked at Jack over her shoulder. "What now?" she asked.

"I guess we climb off," said Jack.

"But then what?" Annie asked sadly. "Where does he go?"

"That's a good question," said Jack.

"He comes with us, of course," someone said.

Jack and Annie gasped.

Balor and Grinda slunk out from behind the tree. Balor carried the black rope.

Jack was stunned. "How—how did you get here so fast?" he asked.

"We took the A train," said Balor. "'Tis actually

a bit faster than riding a unicorn." The boy laughed meanly.

"Shut up, Balor," said Grinda. Then she turned to Jack and Annie. "I am glad you had a happy little ride. But you can say good-bye to Dianthus now. We will take him from here."

"No, you won't!" said Annie.

"Stay away from us!" said Jack.

"Come on, Dianthus, let's go!" said Annie.

Before Dianthus could move, Grinda rushed forward and grabbed his collar with both hands. The unicorn snorted and shook his head. Grinda clung fiercely to the collar. "Get the rope over his head, Balor!" she yelled. "Now!"

Balor looped the black rope into a noose again. The unicorn twisted and turned his head.

Jack kicked at Balor. "Stop!" he yelled. "Get away from us!" Jack felt stupid just yelling and kicking, but he didn't know what else to do.

As Balor and Grinda struggled to get the noose over the unicorn's head, Annie pointed at them. In a loud voice, she shouted:

Fowl of air, appear now here!
Aka-aka-aka-mere!

The black rope fell to the snow. Balor and Grinda started to spin around. They spun like two spinning tops. As they spun, they grew smaller and smaller. Jack saw a blur of colors: gray and brown, green and white, a dash of orange, a dash of yellow.

The spinning slowly came to a stop. The two scary teenagers were gone. In their place were two small mallard ducks.

CHAPTER NINE

It's *Them*!

One duck was gray with black and white markings. The other had a glossy green head and a rust-colored chest. Both had orange webbed feet and long yellow bills. *Quack, quack,* they said.

Annie looked over her shoulder at Jack. "I memorized the duck rhyme a while ago," she said with a grin. "I knew it would come in handy someday."

Jack laughed. "Good work," he said.

The two ducks waddled around on their bright orange feet, quacking. Answering cries came from overhead. A flock of ducks was flying through the clear November sky.

"Go on, Balor and Grinda!" Annie shouted to the two mallards. "Go with them now!"

The mallards quacked at Annie.

"Go on!" Jack chimed in. "Fly south for the winter! You'll have fun! We promise!"

The two mallards quacked and flapped their wings. First one and then the other rose off the ground. They flew high into the sky. Jack held his breath as he watched the mallards soar away, flying south over New York City.

Annie put her arms around the unicorn's neck. Then she rested her head on his silky white mane. "You're safe now," she said. "But you have to leave us. I have to show you the way to Camelot. The problem is, I don't know how to do that."

AH-U-GA! AH-U-GA!

Jack looked over at an avenue that bordered the park. A big yellow taxi was parked by the curb. The driver was honking his horn. He waved through the window.

"What's that guy want?" said Annie, sitting up.

"I don't know," said Jack.

The driver jumped out of the car. He wore a cap and a plaid scarf. "Hey, it's the same driver who deserted us outside the Cloisters," said Annie.

The passenger door of the taxi opened, and a girl stepped out. She was wearing a purple shawl. "And that's the girl who told us to get off at the wrong subway stop," said Jack.

The taxi driver and the girl in the shawl both waved at Jack and Annie. Then the driver lifted his cap and pulled down his scarf. He had red curly hair and a wonderfully familiar grin.

The girl pulled the shawl off her head. Beautiful long black curls fell down to her waist.

"It's *them*!" said Jack.

"Teddy! Kathleen!" Annie shouted.

Jack and Annie slid off the unicorn's back onto

the snowy ground. The young enchanters ran across the snow to them. Annie threw her arms around Teddy. Kathleen threw her arms around Jack. The four of them laughed and talked at the same time.

"That was *you*!"

"That was *you*!"

"That was *us*!"

"I'm sorry I told you to get off at the wrong stop," said Kathleen. "But Teddy was waiting for you there!"

"And I'm sorry I left you stranded in the storm," said Teddy. "But I knew you'd find your way to the Cloisters!"

"We thought you guys were these two kids following us, Balor and Grinda!" said Annie.

"Yes, we just saw you turn them into ducks!" said Kathleen. "Brilliant!"

"Who were they?" asked Jack.

"Apprentices of the Dark Wizard," said Kathleen. "We didn't know they were following you! Even *Merlin* didn't know."

"They were pretty creepy," said Jack.

"Yeah, but they actually helped us without meaning to," said Annie. "They knew the unicorn's name."

"We thought it was *Divine Flower of Rome,*" said Jack.

"I told Merlin that clue might be a bit difficult," said Teddy. "Divine Flower is *dianthus* in Latin, the language of old Rome."

"So do Grinda and Balor know Latin?" asked Annie.

"Hardly," said Teddy. "The unicorn's name is famous throughout the Otherworld. He is known for his great magic."

"And for his goodness," added Kathleen.

"We know about his goodness," said Annie. "When he ran through the streets with his horn in the air, the blizzard ended. And everyone we passed cheered up and seemed to get more hopeful."

"The Dark Wizard was trying to capture Dianthus so he could keep the unicorn's good magic from the rest of the world," said Kathleen. "Merlin will be very pleased that you have foiled the wizard's plan."

"In truth, I believe he would like to thank you himself," said Teddy. He turned toward the yellow taxi parked by the curb.

The back door of the car opened, and two grown-ups stepped out: a tall, elegant woman wearing a wine-colored cloak and a man in a dark blue robe. The man had a long white beard. The woman had long white hair.

"Morgan! Merlin!" whispered Jack.

As the wizard and magical librarian of Camelot walked across the snow, Dianthus stepped forward to greet them. He bowed his head. Merlin tenderly stroked the unicorn's white neck.

Morgan le Fay turned to Jack and Annie. "Hello," she said, smiling. "It is good to see you both." Her lovely voice washed over Jack like music.

"You too," said Annie, hugging the enchantress.

"What are you and Merlin doing here?" Jack asked.

"I have always wanted to visit New York City," said Morgan. "Teddy has just given us quite a ride in that taxi. Merlin had to tell him to slow down several times." Morgan laughed and turned toward Merlin.

"Quite a ride indeed," said Merlin. "Greetings to you both, Jack and Annie."

"Greetings," they said.

"Thank you for saving my beloved Dianthus," said Merlin. "Long ago, he was stolen from Camelot by evildoers. He was rescued by magic weavers in the Netherlands. To keep him safe, they used their art to hide him in their tapestries. I knew I could entrust you two to set him free on the day the spell was to end. But your mission turned out to be more dangerous than I intended. I did not know the Dark Wizard had sent his apprentices to follow you and capture the unicorn."

"Poor Grinda and Balor," said Annie. "Now they're ducks."

"Oh, do not worry," said Teddy. "The spell will wear off in a few days, and they'll find their way home."

"Yes," said Kathleen, "and I am sure the Dark Wizard will have some other wicked plan for them."

"Aye," said Merlin, "but they will no longer have the use of their black rope." He picked the rope up from the ground and handed it to Teddy.

"Take this back to Camelot and see that it is destroyed."

"Gladly," said Teddy.

"It must be terrible to work for the Dark Wizard," said Annie. She looked at Merlin. "I'm glad we work for you instead."

Merlin smiled. "And so am I," he said. "On your last four missions, you and Jack have proved you know how to use magic wisely. And

for that, I now entrust you with one of Camelot's greatest treasures."

Merlin pulled a spiraled wand from his robe. "I give you the Wand of Dianthus," he said. "As you can see, the wand is made in the shape of the unicorn's horn. It has a bit of his magic in it." Merlin held the silver wand out to Jack and Annie.

Jack took the wand from Merlin. It burned in his hand—with cold or warmth, he couldn't tell which.

"With the help of the wand, you can make your own magic," said Merlin.

"But you can only use it after you have tried your hardest," said Morgan, "and remember that it can only be used for another's good."

"We'll remember," breathed Annie.

"Thank you," said Jack. He unbuckled his briefcase and carefully placed the silver wand inside.

"We must leave you now," said Merlin. He turned to Teddy and Kathleen. "You may ride Dianthus home to Camelot. I will be along shortly. But first, I would like to drive that taxi around New York City myself. Morgan, will you join me?"

"Indeed," said Morgan. "But drive a bit more slowly than Teddy, please."

"I promise nothing," said Merlin. He looked

at Jack and Annie. "Good evening to you, my friends. I will call for you again soon."

"Bye," said Annie and Jack.

Merlin took Morgan's arm, and the two walked back to the taxi and climbed into the front seat. The big yellow car sputtered and then took off wildly. As it careened up the avenue, Merlin blew its horn.

AH-U-GA! AH-U-GA!

CHAPTER TEN

The Wand of Dianthus

Jack, Annie, Teddy, and Kathleen laughed.

"My," said Kathleen. "I believe I would much rather ride Dianthus than go with Merlin!"

The white unicorn knelt in the snow. Kathleen and Teddy climbed onto his back. Dianthus stood up.

Teddy smiled down at Jack and Annie. "You know 'tis a very great honor to be given the Wand of Dianthus," he said.

"I know," said Jack shyly. "Thanks for getting us to the right place at the right time today."

"Hey, were you guys in Venice, looking out for us there, too?" said Annie. "And Baghdad? And Paris?"

The two young enchanters looked at one another. Then they nodded their heads.

"We knew it!" said Annie. "Thanks for helping us!"

"And thanks for the book of magic rhymes," said Jack.

"You are most welcome," said Teddy. "And now we must go. We hope to see you again soon."

"Good-bye, Dianthus," said Annie. She stroked the unicorn's neck one last time.

Dianthus lowered his head and stared at her with his soft blue eyes. They sparkled in the last bit of daylight. Annie stood on her toes and whispered in the unicorn's ear. Then she stepped back.

Dianthus snorted. He raised his head. Then he leapt forward. In a flash of silver, the unicorn and his two riders were gone.

Standing in the cold dusk, Annie stared silently into the distance.

"What did you say to him?" asked Jack.

"I told him he had to go with Teddy and Kathleen," Annie said. She blinked back tears. "I told him they would show him the way home now."

"Oh," said Jack. He put his hand on Annie's back. "Don't worry. We'll see Dianthus again someday. I just feel it."

Annie smiled. "You're starting to sound like me," she said.

"Uh-oh," said Jack. He shivered. Night was falling fast. "Ready?"

"Sure, let's go," said Annie. She followed Jack to the tree house and up the rope ladder. They climbed inside and looked out the window.

The lights of New York City were starting to come on. A full moon was rising over the snow-covered park.

"Hello, blue moon," said Jack.

"Good-bye, blue moon," said Annie.

Jack picked up the scroll from Merlin. He pointed to the words *Frog Creek* in Merlin's note. "I wish we could go home!" he said.

The wind started to blow.

The tree house started to spin.

It spun faster and faster.

Then everything was still.

Absolutely still.

❄ ✳ ❄

A cold wind blew through the Frog Creek woods. A few fat snowflakes drifted into the tree house. Jack and Annie were dressed in their own clothes again. Jack's briefcase had turned back into a backpack.

Jack quickly opened the pack and looked inside. "Good," he said. "The Wand of Dianthus is still there."

"Should we take it home with us?" asked Annie.

"I think so," said Jack. "We can keep it safe

until our next mission." He pulled Teddy and Kathleen's book of rhymes out of his pack.

"I guess we can keep our book of rhymes as a souvenir," Jack said. "We won't be using it anymore since we've used up all the rhymes." He stuffed the book back into his backpack.

"We haven't used *all* of them," said Annie. "We still have one left, remember? *Find a Treasure You Must Never Lose.*"

"Oh, I already used that one," said Jack. "Come on, let's go." He grabbed his pack and started down the rope ladder.

"What do you mean you already used that one?" Annie said as she followed him down. "When did you use *that* rhyme?"

Jack stepped onto the ground. "How do you think I found you when you got lost in Central Park?" he said.

"Wait, you thought *I* was a treasure?" said Annie.

Jack shrugged. "I guess," he said. "At least today I did."

Annie smiled. "Cool," she said. "Thanks for finding me when you got lost."

"Not me, *you*," said Jack. "You're the one who got lost."

"No, *you*," said Annie.

"*You*," said Jack.

"Youyouyouyouyou!" said Annie.

Jack laughed. "Whatever," he said. "Let's go have some of Dad's hot chocolate."

The snow began to fall harder. As the cold wind rattled the bare trees of the Frog Creek woods, Jack and Annie hurried home.

More Facts for Jack and Annie and You!

The Great Depression: Today, older New Yorkers remember the Great Depression as one of the most difficult times in the city's history. Lasting from 1929 to about 1939, the Depression was a time when all of America, as well as much of Europe, suffered terrible economic problems that caused many people to lose their jobs.

Subways: Today, millions of people ride the New York subways every day. There are over 400 miles of tracks. Riders no longer drop coins or tokens into a slot in the turnstiles, though. They now slide a MetroCard through an electronic card reader.

Central Park: Today, more than 250,000 people might visit Central Park on a warm weekend and picnic, jog, skate, bicycle, listen to music, or walk dogs. Designed over 150 years ago, Central Park was the first major park created entirely for public use. Its designers, Frederick Law Olmsted and Calvert Vaux, believed that nature could lift the spirits of city dwellers and bring together people from all walks of life.

Belvedere Castle: Today, Belvedere Castle in Central Park serves as a nature observatory. If you live in New York City, you have often heard on TV or radio: "The temperature in Central Park is . . . " That information is coming from the weather instruments that are still housed in the castle.

John D. Rockefeller: Today, America remembers John D. Rockefeller as once being the richest man in the country. After founding the Standard Oil Company, he focused on giving away half of his fortune. Through Rockefeller's generosity, a small museum in Fort Tryon Park in the northern part of the city was acquired by the Metropolitan Museum of Art. That museum is known as the Cloisters.

The Cloisters: Today, the Cloisters is filled with approximately 5,000 works of medieval art, including many works from Rockefeller's own medieval art collection, such as the famous Unicorn Tapestries.

Unicorns: Today, unicorns appear in old stories from countries all over the world, most notably China, India, and medieval Europe. There is no proof that unicorns ever actually existed, though. The only land animal with a single horn is a rhinoceros.

Illustrator's Note

I have illustrated all the Magic Tree House books, but illustrating *Blizzard of the Blue Moon* has been the most enjoyable so far.

My research for this project brought back many fond memories because as a student I often visited many of the places mentioned in the story, especially in Central Park, where I loved to sketch.

Since I still live close to New York City, I came to the city several times and followed the same route that Jack and Annie took from Central Park to the Cloisters.

Many of the places in the story are not very

different than they were in 1938, and I was able to sketch and photograph them. The taxis and the subway trains have changed, but I was able to find pictures of these in books.